MW01716344

MEN AFTER *Midnight*

MARIANNE LACROIX

Ellora's Cave
Romantica Publishing

What the critics are saying...

ETERNAL EMBRACE

4 1/2 Stars "I loved Ms. Lacroix sexy vampire story. She made me want to read more…I must confess: I had not read the first one but I will, there is no question! *Eternal Embrace* is well written and Marianne Lacroix's story is balanced between emotion, passion and strong characters. I am definitively hooked on her and I will follow her career." ~ *ECataRomance Reviews*

DESCENDANTS OF DARKNESS

5 Nymphs and a Recommended Read "LaCroix has done it once again with vividly bringing all the characters in *Descendants of Darkness* to life like few authors can do. Not only are the characters and story line excellent and very detailed, but the sex scenes are about as hot as you'll find anywhere."

~ *Literary Nymphs Reviews*

4 1/2 Kisses "Marianne LaCroix is a talented author who has combined four intriguing stories into one superb novel. From one short novella to the next, I couldn't put the book down. From compelling characters, dangerous situations, to murder and mayhem, each character has to overcome both internal and external conflicts to gain the love of their mates…I will definitely be looking for this authors work in the future."
~ *Romance Divas Reviews*

An Ellora's Cave Romantica Publication

www.ellorascave.com

Men After Midnight

ISBN 9781419958618

Edited by Kelli Kwiatkowski.
Cover art by Syneca.

This book printed in the U.S.A.

Trade paperback Publication March 2009

MEN AFTER MIDNIGHT

ETERNAL EMBRACE

Chapter One

"You must travel south to Paris and claim your mate, Johann. Beneath the city lies a dark underground coven of vampires led by their mistress, Kira." He paused then added, "The Mistress of Midnight is your destiny." The oracle of his coven sat before the firelight, which flickered against his ancient face, ragged and creased. If the man wasn't an immortal vampire, one would suspect the oracle was near his end.

"I have to go to Paris to find my life-mate?" Johann Wilhelm asked incredulously. He disliked the idea immediately, having sour memories of Paris from centuries before.

"Yes, and that's where you will stay," the vampire said as he gazed down at his runes, stones and bones thrown in the ancient method of Nordic fortune-telling and divination.

"Live there in Paris? I have no wish to leave here to live with some woman and her French underground vampires."

"You are destined to lead the covens, join them together and rule with intelligence and strength. Many will look to you and your mate for guidance. The union will become one of power and passion."

"Passion?"

The old vampire nodded. "Johann, the vampiress Kira is your destiny. With her you will find a love that defies time, and a passion all-consuming."

Ever since his turning Johann had wandered the earth longing for his life-mate. Any hope of truly finding her had begun to fade a century ago.

It had been a long time since that night in the land of Eire when he was attacked by the vampire Rourke. His brother Lucius had pleaded for their lives, and they both became descendants of darkness—vampires.

After studying the ways of the vampire from the creature who created them, Lucius and Johann traveled Europe for centuries, finally parting ways in Romania. Lucius remained in that dark country to serve in the army of Vlad Tepes III, and Johann traveled home to Norway.

Johann had missed his homeland. Of course, the people he had known prior were long dead. He had accumulated wealth in his travels, enough to finance a rich lifestyle, and Johann proceeded to build a castle retreat. In doing so, he attracted other vampires existing in the Northlands. There they gathered and formed a coven of immortals. Johann brought safety and prosperity to his people, and leadership to an otherwise unorganized group.

"I can't leave the coven behind," Johann started. "They look to me for guidance." Part of him was scrambling for excuses to stay. He had built his home here and for the past centuries it had been his haven. Within the walls of Wilhelm Castle, Johann found peace. However, lately, he began to feel the emptiness in his heart. He longed for love, a purpose to his very existence.

"You will come back, Johann, but your place will be in Paris with your mate." The oracle paused before adding, "Once you meet her, there will be no question to the truth."

Johann was bothered by the oracle's predictions. He retired to his chamber, flopping down on the grand bed covered in rich burgundy velvet. It was lavish and fit his lifestyle.

His lifestyle. How would Kira fit into his lifestyle? He was a man used to taking control in the bedroom. Would a woman who was leader of her own coven submit to his command?

The oracle said there would be no doubts once Johann met her. She was his life-mate, or so the ancient vampire claimed.

Memories of Paris raced to mind at the mere mention of its name. It was there he'd come face-to-face with love. While traveling with Lucius, they'd stayed there, hunting the streets for their meals. Of course, the more risqué side of the city appealed to them both. Picking up willing women to sate their hunger for sex and blood was easy.

It was while in Paris that he learned women generally used love for their own purposes. He had discovered this the hard way, and it was now his long-held opinion that women were good for only one thing—sex.

And he used women for sex, as did Lucius. Many times in their travels they shared women. Nights of heated ecstasy, bringing fantasies to life for their victims—their last living moments filled with pleasure.

It had been a long time since Johann had shared a woman with his brother. After splitting ways centuries before, he'd not seen Lucius since. His brother refused to return to the Northlands for any reason. Memories of his human life there were too painful for that vampire to bear.

Not even Lucius was immune from the pain of love and loss.

Lying in bed, Johann sighed. "I will never love this Kira. I will have her body and soul. I will possess her, but she will never have my heart."

He let his mind rest as he slipped into the deathlike sleep of his kind.

* * * * *

The mist of dreams shaded over his senses. He awoke within darkness. A fire nearby crackled, the flames taking the edge off the cool air within the room. But it did little to ease the cold that settled through his body.

"Rest, my lord. Let me comfort you, warm you," a woman said as she neared him, the orange-red flickering light caressing her glowing skin. By the gods, she was perfect.

Johann was faced with the most beautiful woman he'd ever seen. Hair black as midnight and eyes green as emeralds, she was his vision of...*perfection*. She smiled and his blood heated.

"Who are you?"

"I am a dream."

He glanced around and didn't recognize anything. Before he could ask where he was or why he was there, she closed her mouth over his. She tasted of ambrosia and the finest wine. Her lips were firm and plump, made for kissing.

His cock stirred to life and it was then he realized he lay naked upon a pallet of furs. The floor and walls were made of stone, like those of a medieval castle, but different from his Northland retreat. He couldn't clearly make out the tapestries on the walls but it mattered little to him. Right now, all he wanted was the skilled touch of this woman upon his body.

She briefly grasped his length within her hand and he moaned. "You *must* be a dream."

"A vision...of love, my lord," she breathed against his mouth.

Her body was inviting and curvaceous, and as her breasts glided along his chest, he gave in to the desire she invoked.

She was an expert with her mouth, teasing him with each flick of her pink tongue against his skin. She tantalized one hard nipple then the other, and lightly clawed at his sides with her fingernails. The wicked sensation heightened his awareness of her naked figure rubbing so softly along his hardened body.

"Close your eyes, my lord, and let me pleasure you."

Johann sighed and relaxed his eyelids, giving himself over to her ministrations.

She teased his balls with her fingers, then leaned in and licked their surface. He groaned as she tasted him. He wished she'd touch his hard cock again as it bobbed before her face in enticement. To have those luscious lips curl around his length was what he yearned for, what he craved.

Suddenly he realized he was hungry. Blood—he needed her blood. Even the dream of the feast was enough to drive his libido into a frenzy. He wanted—no, needed—to taste her blood upon his tongue, to take in the liquid life-fluid that pumped through her veins. Oh, how she must taste—delicious and succulent.

She began to run her tongue up his cock, from base to tip. At the small opening of the purplish head, she dipped her tongue into the fluid seeping from the hole.

He was in agony. He was in ecstasy. When she closed her mouth around his cock he flexed his hips, driving himself deeper into her. He slipped his fingers into her hair, gently guiding her head over his penis, encouraging each suckling movement of her mouth.

She took him deep into her mouth and down her throat. He'd never experienced such utopia at the hands, and mouth, of a woman before. Yes, he'd been sucked by many, many women in the past, but somehow this was different—unique. She was completely enraptured by her task, and the little moans of pleasure within her throat only made his cock harder. The vibrations of her sounds drove him closer to the edge.

The climax built within Johann and it wouldn't take much more for him to explode into her sweet mouth.

Once again she caressed his balls, massaging the sac with her fingertips, scraping her nails lightly over the sensitive surface. When she pressed a finger behind the sac, he screamed.

There was no holding back the orgasm that she induced. He sprayed his heated seed into her mouth and down her throat, and she drank at it hungrily.

But it wasn't enough. He reached down to one of her clawing hands and grasped her wrist. As he continued to pump semen into her, he brought her wrist to his mouth and bit down. The lovely, salty richness of her blood exploded over his tongue and down his throat. Yes, her blood was the essence of life he'd longed for throughout the centuries.

She continued to massage and urge out his cum, and she lapped it up with enthusiastic delight. When he finally released her wrist, licking the wound to close it, she eased her mouth off his cock. Immediately, he was saddened at the loss of her heat about him. It was like he was no longer connected to her—a connection he realized was deeper than a mere dream.

He lay back, his head resting against the soft furs, and he sighed. "What's your name, my sweet?"

"Kira, my lord." Her voice was a faint echo through the darkness as the vision faded.

Kira, the Mistress of Midnight.

It was a sign.

Johann sank into the depths of sexual satisfaction and contentment, but before he succumbed, he decided a trip to Paris was definitely in store.

Kira was about to become more than a specter in his dreams. He had to see her—touch her—in the flesh.

Chapter Two

The sun dipped below the horizon, painting the sky brilliant oranges and reds, a spectacular natural backdrop to one of man's greatest architectural feats, the *Tour Eiffel*. The silhouette of the black steel structure was a stark contrast to the dance of light and colors against the low-hanging clouds.

Paris came alive at night with its legendary electric display. Tourists flocked there year 'round to gaze upon the Seine from the famous Jules Verne restaurant which rose high above the city within the Eiffel Tower.

Some would visit the *Arc de Triomphe* and pay tribute to the former French Emperor Napoleon. Still others didn't bother to discover the city's magnificent treasures. Such visitors would skip the *Louvre*, the greatest collection of art in the world. What a waste. France had so much to offer visitors and many didn't see beyond the busy streets filled with shops for the tourists. Daylight was wasted on such mortal creatures.

But Kira didn't belong to the light. There was a life of darkness in Paris located beneath the bustling streets and towering monuments. A much darker side to this city of lovers thrived in the thousands of tunnels and catacombs built by those who turned from the light centuries ago. There, the vampires existed in a community of darkness.

Kira, a mysterious and powerful woman, ruled this Parisian coven. Her centuries of experience aided her wisdom. That, and her blood connection to the ancient Diablo.

Diablo was the taken name of the creature who snatched Kira into the vampiric world. He was tall, handsome and his voice mesmerized any mortal within its range. His blue eyes entranced with just a glance, and his smile could make a female swoon. To say he was sin incarnate was only touching the surface of his persona. Diablo was a devil who appeared as an angel.

Kira had been captured by his physical beauty, his long black hair falling down around his powerful shoulders and his chiseled features, sculpted by a hand more skilled than that of Michelangelo. She wanted him at first glance, and she gave in to her animalistic needs, only to have him rip away her mortality.

He was a king of their kind, a master of vampires, and she had become his companion. She longed to give her body to him, and he took from her the innocence that he craved. Together they traveled the globe, feasting upon the living and building strength for the centuries to come.

Her purpose through the centuries had remained a mystery until they arrived in Paris. There Diablo revealed his intent—Kira was to become a vampire leader in France. His ancient blood and her immortal bond would aid her in leading one of the largest and most powerful vampire societies on earth.

"It is time for you to fulfill your destiny, Kira my sweet," Diablo whispered to her one night as they stood together, looking out over the Seine. "I love you dearly, and I wish I was meant to become your mate, but alas, it is not to be. Though we enjoyed our time together, you are meant for another."

"I can't believe you will just leave me, Diablo. You held my heart the day I first saw you. We must be mates to have been together these three centuries." She wrapped her arms about his waist, his powerful body arousing hers with its closeness.

"You will know your mate when he appears. It has been foreseen in the future, my Kira. We stole moments of pleasure, but both our destinies lie elsewhere. Yours is here in Paris. Lead the coven with your wisdom and natural commanding presence. When the true master of your heart arrives, you will know it. Your soul will recognize him as the one to rule by your side."

Diablo's words echoed in Kira's mind as she sat alone on her throne, overlooking the reveling vampires celebrating the summer solstice. Many of them remained steadfast to their Pagan beliefs over the centuries. She was one of them. Now the ancient of her coven, she held strong to her mortal beliefs and was among the first creatures to show religious tolerance. The humans were very slow in following suit. Even now, many couldn't bring themselves to allow beliefs that differed from their own.

It was during times like these, when celebration filled the air, that Kira missed Diablo the most. He was right to leave. He wasn't her mate. Nevertheless, she missed him all the same. He had been her friend, her confidant and her lover. She longed to find her true mate, wished him by her side to rule the vampires who turned to her for protection and guidance.

Music filled the air, along with the scent of fresh blood brought in from human donors. There were those among the living who longed for immortality and served the vampires in hopes of finding a way into their society. It was rare that a human servant would ever cross over. The humans served as pets to feast upon, to use to the vampires' benefit. They also guarded the entryways into the vampire lair beneath the Paris streets. At night her clan members were strong, but during the day they needed to seek the darkness below. The human pets watched over their masters and mistresses, ensuring their safety. For centuries, this pyramid society of humans and vampires worked in harmony.

Suddenly a hush echoed through the tunnels as the vampires stopped in their celebrating. A vampire, a stranger to them, had entered the underworld.

The silence was piercing to Kira, who now rose from her throne. The vampires parted to the sides of the large meeting room, illuminated by thousands of thick wax candles. Their flames flickered in the darkness, painting the stone and mortar walls with soft light.

He strode through the parting crowd, tall and muscular. His long blond hair fell free around his shoulders and down his back. His pale skin was flushed from a recent feeding and his clear blue eyes pinned her to the spot. "Gorgeous" was hardly the best word to describe the sexual vitality this vampire emanated. Some of the female vampires in the crowd sighed and felt his magnetism pull to them.

"My lady Kira, let me introduce myself," he said with a Nordic accent. It fit his fair looks, and gave him an Old World suavity and grace. "My name is Lord Johann Wilhelm of the Northlands and of Wilhelm Castle."

"Greetings, my lord. I see you have an advantage over me. I hadn't expected such a distinguished visitor."

"I'm here for a certain purpose."

His voice made her intimate muscles clench in need. Damn, not even Diablo had made her body come alive with such want so fast.

"And what is your reason in coming, Lord Johann?"

He stepped closer and she could smell the spicy scent of his cologne and the tangy blood upon his breath. Her heart leapt in her chest as he stopped mere inches from her. He was dressed impeccably, his fine silk suit—costly and black—fit his tall, powerful frame to perfection.

"I'm here to take you as my mate, Kira," he whispered so only she could hear. He was so close, so intoxicating to her senses.

"What makes you so sure you are my destined mate?"

"Because now that I have seen your beauty, I know that the fates foretold correctly. The oracle of my coven saw you in a vision and proclaimed I was destined to come here for you. Once together, our covens will unite and we shall rule in wisdom and strength. You will be my bride, and I, your husband for all eternity."

Air seemed to have been drawn out of the cavernous room. With him so close, it was as though they were the only ones there. "What if my heart tells me that you are not my mate?"

"You are, sweet Kira. I shall have no other. Once we are joined, I shall worship your body each night. I will conquer your heart. You will be *mine*."

She straightened taller and gazed sharply into his eyes. "My lord, you're presumptuous and arrogant. You cannot order me to join with you. I am mistress here, and in this lair you are my subordinate."

He moved in closer still, towering over her. She could feel the heat pour off his skin through his clothes, calling to her. "Kira, you will learn I am your true lord, and will soon beg for my touch. You will submit to me. We will join as mates and rule as equals, but in our chambers you will freely give me your submission."

Now her stomach somersaulted. Damn, he was presuming too much—and her body liked everything he said. She breathed deeply to calm her own nerves but all it did was fill her senses with his masculine scent.

He leaned toward her, whispering right next to her left ear. His breath was warm and intoxicating upon her skin. "I can smell your sweet honey, my lady. It calls to me as it oozes from your luscious cunt."

"You are not only impertinent, but vulgar. Leave now before I call my security forces to have you escorted from our lair."

"How about we make a deal then? If I win, you let me stay. If not, then I leave without resistance." His tone echoed his self-assurance and ability to win whatever he planned.

How intriguing.

She turned her face to his, still close and alluring, their lips only a breath away. She could already taste him upon her tongue. "What kind of deal?"

"I bet I can make you come without even touching you."

* * * * *

She was the woman from his dream, the temptress who brought his passion to life. He didn't think the flesh-and-blood woman could match the one in his vision.

She was the Mistress of Midnight and he'd come to the end of his search for a life-mate. The oracle was correct—he *did* recognize her as his destined lover.

However, it was obvious Kira was used to playing with men. She was wild, untamable, and he was up to the challenge of mastering her body and her heart.

But what about *his* heart? He'd felt the pain of love and betrayal, and now Johann stood face-to-face with a woman who held the power to destroy him. No—his life-mate would be a companion only. Love was a weak emotion he refused to ever again succumb to. This union was for the good of the covens, nothing more.

He had to prove to her he was her mate, and if he had to use his telekinetic powers to do it, he would. He'd never used his ability to touch through the will of his mind to arouse a woman. Perhaps it was time he did.

With a devilish smile he repeated, "I bet that I can make you come without touching you."

"I don't think that is possible, Lord Johann."

"I love the sound of my name on your lips. Sounds more like a plea for me to fuck you than a mere name," he said, brushing her ear with his lips, following that with a quick nip to her earlobe. "And it is very possible, my lady. I can make that cunt crave for me to fill it and not even lay a finger upon your ivory skin."

Her sharp intake of breath just excited him more. His cock was rock hard and ready to plunge deep into her center. He imagined she'd scream and pant for more as he pumped in and out of her tight, hot sheath.

As much as he wanted to throw her to the floor and fuck her until sunrise, he had to be cautious. Vampires could be dangerous if cornered, especially one as powerful as Kira.

"You underestimate me, my lord. I am no ordinary vampire."

"Indeed? And what secrets do you hold to your heart?"

"I am an ancient of our kind, bonded with the great vampire Diablo."

Johann's eyebrow cocked upward. "Diablo? Yes, I know of him." Diablo preferred to reside in Spain within his own stronghold, and Johann never had reason to cross paths with him.

"I was his companion at one time, long ago," she said.

Johann sniffed the air. A trace of the vampire Diablo hung within the cavern, but nothing recent. "He's not here now."

"No."

"It matters not, my sweet Kira. You will be mine. I will carry you kicking and screaming to your bed to show you that your destiny is parallel with mine."

"You wouldn't dare," she growled.

Chuckling low, he whispered, "Oh yes I would."

A large panther growled behind him. Johann turned to see that two giant vampires had shifted into black panthers, both ready to pounce. In their cat forms, these two would be dangerous—even to him.

Kira raised her hand and halted the guards' advance. They were obviously her means of disposing unwelcome visitors.

"You're causing my friends to become nervous."

"Then perhaps we should retire to a more private area so we may discuss our deal."

"I don't make deals. My word is law here. There will be no deal."

He leaned into her again, able to taste her skin with a small flick of his tongue to her neck. He could smell her excitement, along with the increased blood flow running through her veins. The sound of her heart beating fast, combined with the unmistakable scent of her cream, made him groan. "I promise to make you glad that you did."

She stood silently, but her body was on fire in reaction to his nearness. He sensed her body heat rising with each passing moment, her heartbeat quickening with each breath. Even through her black blouse he saw her nipples pebble into hardened points, aching for his mouth to claim their berrylike surface.

"Don't make me carry you, Kira. I meant what I said."

Her gaze slid to his face. "And I won't be so easy to convince, my lord."

"We will see."

* * * * *

Kira knew she was completely out of her mind. She hardly ever indulged in sex unless it was with Diablo, but this vampire made her want to abandon caution.

Here she was, closing the door to her private chambers, alone with a master of a clan of vampires, one as powerful as she. Kira turned to him and saw him fighting the beast within. He was just as turned on.

"Do we have a deal, my lady?" he asked in a voice that was smooth as melted chocolate, and just as delicious.

"Does it bother you that I was the consort of such an ancient and powerful vampire as Diablo?"

"No, not really. You haven't been with him for a long time." He paused then asked, "Why did he leave?"

"He said I was meant for another."

"That would be me."

"No, I don't believe it."

"You should be able to sense that we are meant for each other." He moved in closer and added, "I want to make love to you. Here. Now."

"What of our deal?"

"I thought you didn't make deals."

By the gods, he was driving her crazy with desire. She wanted him to suck on her clit, make sensual music using her as his instrument.

"I may have changed my mind." She paused and flashed him a small smile. "Go ahead. Make me come. But, you *can't* touch me."

"Your wish is my command, my love," he said huskily.

Then she watched him position himself before her, several feet away. There was a knowing smile on his face and before she could ask what he intended, she felt hands upon her body. The touch was preternatural and—*oh, dear Lord, sinful!*

"Can you feel me, sweet Kira?" he asked with a chuckle as she watched him flick his tongue from where he stood. She felt the sensation instantly on her nipple.

She inhaled sharply as his tongue laved at her breast, causing the nipple to harden and elongate. Moaning, she knew her strategy had failed. He *could* make her come without physically touching her.

"Since the moment I smelled your perfume upon the winds, drawing me here to you, I've longed for this moment."

It was as though several hands stroked her, bypassing her clothes and touching her skin. One hand cupped her breast as his phantom tongue feasted on its sweetness. Another hand cupped her bottom, and still two others trailed down the backs of her thighs and calves. At her ankles, his thumbs traced small circles upon the sensitive skin. Fingertips moved upward and she gasped as another hand grasped her other breast and teased the nipple into a point.

Never had she felt such worshipful hands—and ghostly hands at that. It was like being pleasured by several men at once.

Then he touched her weeping center, parting her folds to caress the button that would bring her into paradise. No, not his finger—his tongue stroked the throbbing center of her being, teasing her clit, and she moaned, unable to hold back the ecstasy building within her body.

"Oh, sweet Kira, you are ambrosia to this hungry vampire." His voice only added to the ripples of pleasure now skittering across her skin and the excitement pumping with each heartbeat.

She threw back her head and an ethereal purr escaped her throat.

This stranger had awakened the beast she kept at bay in her soul. Within moments of their meeting, she was climbing into a dangerous situation. She raged with need—a need to mate with this incredible man. She tried to tell herself he was just another alpha vampire, but her body didn't listen. With the touch of his tongue to her straining clit, she lost all reason. Nothing could prevent her from giving into his phantom ministrations.

With another pass of his tongue and a squeeze of his hand upon her breast, she dropped down onto her knees. She opened her thighs and reached down to her center. Even through the material of her tight black leggings, her moisture was evident.

"I need you now, Johann. Please, fuck me before I die from want." Her voice was a whisper as she pleaded with him.

Then the sensation of his mouth closing on her clit shot through her entire being. He sucked at the flesh and all restraint was broken. She climaxed violently as he touched her with his powers. Hands teased and caressed each part of her as his mouth worked magic upon her bud.

Her body convulsed, sending floods of joy surging through her veins. The beast clawed to the surface and she screamed with the mating call of her kind. The walls echoed her song as her body rode the waves over and over.

As the contractions ebbed, she reclined onto her back, lying upon the floor. Never had she had such an intense climax, and without the benefit of a cock fucking her. By the gods, this man was a dream lover. What would it be like once his flesh really touched hers?

"I won the bet," he said from across the room.

She glanced up to him, standing there in her chambers. He had peeled away his clothes and stood gloriously naked. Hard muscle and sinew graced his tall figure. Damn, he was perfection. His blond hair was a beautiful complement to his pale skin. His cornflower-blue eyes were heated and intense as his gaze roamed over her body. It was as though he stripped her with those eyes.

"You won the bet, Johann. Now you have me. What do you propose to do with me?" Her voice was thick with sexual excitement, husky and seductive. She hardly recognized herself.

"I'm going to fuck you and make you scream for more."

"And then?" she panted.

"Then we will rule together as it has been foretold."

"I won't be weak before my people."

"I would never want you to be. Only in the privacy of our bedchambers will you be submissive to my touch."

He crossed the room and stood above her. She felt completely at his mercy, just as he wished. Somehow it was not at all unpleasant. On the contrary, she liked letting down her defenses and allowing him to take charge. There was something irresistibly sexy about letting this man take control...becoming her lord and master.

As he looked down upon her figure sprawled on the floor, she felt powerful. In his eyes she saw the intensity of his passion, and his rock-hard cock stood proud and erect from the blond nest at his groin. He was very aroused by her.

She smiled and slowly ran the tip of her tongue over her top lip, testing his reaction. His cock jumped at her subtle action, and she felt the true power in her submissive position. She enjoyed his lust-filled gaze raking over her body and she wanted more. She needed to have him inside her, filling her core with his flesh, joining them in the ancient dance of mates.

Diablo had taught her the ways between men and women centuries ago, but it was an empty experience. Only now could she admit that they had used each other to sate the sexual hunger, as well as the sensual blood thirst that accompanied the act. This time, she felt something more than she ever experienced with Diablo. Johann was about to complete her. This was going to be more than sex.

Johann reached out to her and said, "Come, sweet Kira. Let us go to bed where we can be much more comfortable."

She took his offered hand and a jolt of heated electricity shot through her arm, coursed through her veins. As she stood, she was aware of her own body's response to this blond Viking warrior. Her pussy was slick with cream from her orgasm but it still felt empty, yearning for him to fill it to the hilt.

He pulled her into his arms and her body pressed against his nakedness. Even through the thin layer of fabric, she felt his burning skin and the molten blood pumping in his veins. *Hot and sexy. Untamable. Irresistible.*

"You feel perfect, but you have too many clothes on."

"My thoughts exactly," she moaned.

A tearing sound and an effortless tug and Johann rid of her blouse and leggings. Kira felt as if she had come home, standing skin to skin within the arms of this vampire. Was this how it felt to have your one true mate?

His lips tasted the soft, creamy skin of her shoulder and her body shuddered beneath his touch. Heated blood surged faster through her body as her heart pounded within.

He whispered words in his native tongue and she stood mesmerized. Melting into his body, she joined him on many levels. Not just physical, but emotional and mental.

Her eyes rolled back as his lips danced across her skin and she sighed at the blissful pleasure from such a simple gesture. Then she was lifted into his arms as he carried her to the bed. Laying her upon the soft down comforter, he quickly covered her soft body with his hard one.

They fit together perfectly. His hands mapped each inch of her skin as he studied her form through taste and touch.

Ecstasy bubbled beneath the surface as her vampiric blood boiled, wanting desperately to mingle with his, the ultimate bond between vampires. Through a sexual exchange of blood and orgasm, they would be united for the rest of time—immortal lovers. To ever break this joining would mean their destruction. Two halves of one whole was achieved with this ritual. She didn't share such a sacred link to her mentor, but her soul cried out for Johann to complete her.

His tongue laved at her erect nipple and a moan escaped her lips. Her hips moved of their own volition and when his fingers dipped into her honeyed folds, she bucked against his palm.

"So slick and sweet, my Mistress of Midnight, you slay me with your responsiveness to my touch."

"I can't help it," she whispered as his thumb stroked her straining clit. A finger entered her wet passage and she nearly fell to pieces.

"Hold off, Kira. Don't come yet. We have an eternity of bliss to explore. Don't rush this."

"But I need you, Johann." Her hips moved in beat with each stroke from his fingers. "Want you..." Dare she tell him how much she truly wanted everything he could give? She desired his heart, body and soul.

His penis was poised outside her entrance and he moaned. "I want you more than anything I've ever known. Fear not, the desire for your sweet body runs deeper than a physical satisfaction." He thrust into her channel, and she cried out as he vowed, "I claim you, Kira. You are mine—heart, body and soul—in exchange for my complete devotion."

She hardly heard him speak as she surrendered to the moment. With his cock deep within her channel, Kira clung to him, his sweat-drenched skin slick against hers. He retreated then thrust back inside, filling her, stretching vaginal walls that formed a perfect fit about his length.

She wanted more, to feel more, to be completely absorbed by Johann as he took her.

He pulled out slightly only to slam into her again. Control was fleeting as his tempo increased. She flexed her hips to meet his thrusts before arching her back to keep her hips still, in perfect position as he pumped repeatedly in and out of her wet entrance.

She couldn't hold back. Her body began to convulse in orgasm and she cried out as he plunged deeper into her. Colors spun about her as if she were tumbling in a kaleidoscope. She gripped his shoulders as she rode out her climax, yet he continued to move at a frenzied pace.

She screamed aloud as another climax rocked her entire world. Crashes of emotions, her own as well as Johann's, flooded her brain. They were exchanging memories in the midst of orgasm. Only then was she aware of the sharp pain at her neck. As Johann pumped his seed into her womb, he drank from her the rich essence of her blood. Each drawing of blood from her vein sent her higher into orgasm, one climax crashing into another as her body celebrated this animalistic and bestial intimacy, and her heart sang in joy at the sheer unbelievable euphoria.

"Johann, yes, take me…claim me," she panted as he emptied the last of his seed into her body.

* * * * *

It was the moment he had awaited his entire existence. She succumbed to his loving such as none had ever before. His heart nearly burst when he entered her tight sheath and she moaned beneath him. She was his mate for all eternity, and when he sipped her life elixir, his anger and pain from the past were wiped away. Drinking from her luscious neck, he transferred his memories, beginning the bonding ritual of true mates.

He slipped out of her body and immediately missed the wet heat. She whimpered at the loss too. "Soon, Kira. We shall be joined again soon," he whispered, then kissed her forehead gently. Who would have known he held such tenderness within him, after all these centuries of living as a vampire?

"I can't believe this is happening," she mused softly.

"Neither can I. Such emotions are foreign to me, but with you it seems natural, completely right."

She gazed up into his face in wonderment. "I feel the same."

Johann inexplicably found himself wondering about Kira's last companion. He was amazed at the twinge of jealousy that surfaced as he wondered briefly if she thought of Diablo at all now.

Her fingertips traced his jaw and she reassured, "Johann, my heart is yours. I think you know that already." Then he heard within his mind, *"Everything that I am belongs to you, my Viking lord."*

Kissing her was his response. He plunged into her mouth as though denied sustenance for a century and he drank her into his soul. Her tongue met his in a sensual dance and he moaned in ecstasy.

Her mind brushed across his in a loving caress and he relished the sensation. It was a much more intimate connection than the physical, sexual bond. Nothing he ever experienced could match the pleasurable touch of her thoughts reaching out to him.

He broke the kiss then muttered, "We must make sure your coven accepts me as your husband."

She nodded, and as he lifted himself off her, he missed their closeness already. Skin to skin was the only way he wanted to be with Kira. *She will be naked and beneath me every time we are in our chambers,* he thought. *But then again, having her ride me is a nice image too.*

"I heard that," she laughed, slipping from the bed and padding across the room to her armoire, where she pulled out a red silk robe.

He pulled on his discarded pants and smiled. "Having you read my thoughts…I'll have to get used to that."

Striding over to her, he took her into his arms, relishing the feel of cool silk against his skin and the heat radiating from her skin beneath.

Kira felt secure and safe within his arms, and the connection they now shared was not only pleasurable but euphoric.

Then a pounding at the door broke the moment.

Chapter Three

"Kira! Another stranger is here!" one of her servants yelled in a panicked voice.

She only had half a second for the information to sink in before the door opened soundlessly, and another vampire waltzed past the servant and into the room.

"Lucius," Johann said calmly.

Kira was stuck to the spot by the uncanny resemblance of this vampire to Johann. It was as though they were…brothers?

Lucius was massive, slightly taller than Johann. He was handsome and commanding, a true leader, powerful and dominant. Johann and Lucius shared the same pale blond hair falling free and straight down their backs, as well as the same clear blue eyes.

Kira's body reacted at the sight of the two gorgeous men, two alphas within her bedroom. Her pussy ached and her nipples tightened at her next thought. Only in fantasies would she entertain two men at once. While with Diablo all those years ago, he had asked her to experience a threesome but she'd refused, opting to watch as he took another woman before her. But now with her mate, her true mate, Kira was yearning to experience something new, something exciting.

"What are you doing here?" Johann asked, placing himself between her and the newcomer.

"I sensed you the moment you entered Paris. I…I wanted to see you. It has been so long—centuries."

Johann nodded. "You never came home."

"No."

"I understand why you stayed away."

Lucius neared and the powerful vampire seemed almost vulnerable. "It's no excuse. I neglected you, my brother. I missed you."

Johann seemed to consider his brother's brief apology. "Never in the centuries since we parted did you even consider coming home?"

Lucius clasped Johann at the shoulders, a firm grip but not menacing. "I couldn't. The thought of everything I left behind…I couldn't. Please, can you ever forgive my absence?"

For a moment a chill settled over the room and Kira shivered, but then Johann smiled warmly and embraced his brother. "I should have left home and looked for you."

"Let's just promise not to let a few more centuries pass before seeing each other again," Lucius said as they parted.

Kira stared in amazement. So alike, yet so different. She sensed a slight bitterness within Lucius, a force driven by pain. He hid his emotions well, but with his brother so close the strong vampire's resolve weakened slightly and his past shone from within.

As though hearing her thoughts, Lucius turned his attention to Kira. "You're strong—very unique." He cocked a brow as she clutched her robe at the throat.

"Diablo told me of your beauty. I should have come sooner, perhaps beating my brother to your lovely body." Lucius stepped closer and Johann wrapped an arm about her, enclosing her in his warmth.

Lucius stared at her, and as his eyes slowly traveled over her scantily clad body, her heart skipped a beat.

"Her heart is not up for grabs to the highest bidder." The possessiveness in Johann's voice warned his brother of the depth of their connection.

"Perhaps not," Lucius muttered. Heat filled his eyes and she gasped at the intensity. Want, desire and sexual ecstasy reflected within those beautiful eyes as he looked at her.

"She's mine, Lucius. Don't think you can come here and take her from me." A threat lay beneath Johann's words.

Lucius slowly shook his head. "No, I'm not here to take her from you." A small smile curled his lips. "But she wants me."

A jolt of sexual excitement shot through her. Her breath quickening, she couldn't deny her desire. She did want to have this vampire in her bed. And Johann.

"She wants both of us, brother," Lucius said with a growl as he reached out and touched her face. "Don't you, Kira? You want to have both of us within you, two powerful vampires fucking you until you can't walk. Do not worry, Johann and I have shared our paramours before—many, many times before."

She couldn't speak, not trusting herself to make a sound lest she betrayed her wanton desires.

"We shared women, fucked them, loved them," Johann explained. "By the gods, Kira, I smell your juices as the thought of us sharing you excites you further. You make me want to drink from you, lose myself in loving you," he purred in her ear.

In her other ear, Lucius whispered, "Think of it, Johann and me both inside you, pumping into you as you scream from one climax after another." She whimpered and he continued, "I know it excites you, Kira." He pushed away the thin material of her robe and exposed one of her breasts. At the light brush of his thumb over her nipple, she closed her eyes and sighed.

"Would you like both of us to make love to you, sweet Kira?" Johann asked gently.

She cracked open her eyes and looked at him. "Would it please you?"

"Anything that heightens your arousal pleases me. I want you to know you can live your fantasies with me."

Could she do this, have Johann and Lucius in her bed? What would they think of her for wanting to live this fantasy she refused to voice aloud?

"You must tell us you want us—both." Lucius' voice was on the edge of control and the sound excited her even more.

"Do you want us both within you, Kira, making love to you, fucking you for our pleasure?" Johann nibbled at her throat and she sighed, giving herself over to the sensations of them touching her.

"And *your* pleasure, Kira," Lucius whispered against her earlobe then grazed his fangs lightly along its sensitive surface.

She gave in to their words, their hands upon her body, peeling away the thin silk to reveal her skin to their touch. Her breath quickened, as if she needed the air to survive this sensual assault, but it was nothing more than a long-held human instinct.

Johann knelt upon the floor, his tongue tracing a path down as he lowered himself. Meanwhile Lucius stripped and then stood behind her, pulling her into his powerful embrace. As his hands cupped her breasts, she sighed.

"Tell us that you want us," he tempted, his fingers pinching the hardened points of her nipples.

"I want you," she said breathlessly. "Both of you."

Johann began to kiss her feet, his tongue darting out to lick and taste as he continued. His sensual assault fogged her mind. There was no clear thinking, only sensation as these vampires seduced her.

"Your breasts are perfect, Kira. Responsive to my touch. Does your cunt react each time my thumb passes over your nipple?" Lucius' voice was low and sultry, urging her to express her feelings and growing desires as he caressed her body. Just the sensation of his body behind her, naked and warm, was enough to make her juices flow. His cock was hard and searing hot against her ass, and when he moved his hips slightly to one side, brushing the massive erection along her buttocks, she moaned. Words were unable to form upon her lips.

Johann worked his way up her shin in slow passes of lips on skin. His fingers massaged in small circles as he moved upward with his mouth.

When Johann came closer to her core, she weakened. Lucius licked her neck, nipping her skin between his teeth as he continued to worship her breasts with his hands. Johann lifted one of her legs and leaned her thigh upon his shoulder. Her cunt gaped before him and she panted in anticipation. His warm breath grazed over the pink flesh of her sex as he moved his face closer. Lucius held her securely, and she was aware she'd given complete control over to her two vampire lovers.

And what a glorious surrender it was, to have Lucius and Johann using her body for their pleasure, and granting her pleasure in return.

Johann dipped a finger into her folds and she cried out at the sweet sensation. Her clit strained for his touch, aching for the caresses that would send her body into orgasm once again.

"Not so quickly," whispered Lucius from behind her.

It was hard not to buck her hips as Johann tested and teased her reactions with his fingers. Then he spread her labia, exposing the small nubbin that swelled with desire. He leaned in and gently kissed its surface and she tossed her head back against Lucius, succumbing to the moment.

His teeth grazed over her clit and he nibbled.

Her body was on fire. It began at that small pleasure point between her legs that Johann suckled and savored like a morsel to be cherished at length. Liquid heat poured from her slit and ran down the inside of her thigh. She wanted to explode, feeling the blast build from within and spreading through every cell of her body.

"Hold off, Kira, don't come yet," Lucius urged.

Johann's tongue rolled over her clit and she screamed in frustration, fighting to obey his instructions.

Then without a word, Johann pulled away. Lucius scooped her into his arms and carried her close to his body.

"We want to be inside you when you come, dear Kira," Lucius said as he lay her down upon the bed.

She sank into the bed's softness and enjoyed its welcoming comfort. Then the mattress dipped as one of her lovers climbed onto the bed, followed by the other.

Two sexy vampires at once—one was her mate and the other, a lover as enchanting as a wizard casting a spell of seduction. She'd always dreamed of having a ménage, and now was the time. With Johann by her side, it felt right.

Lucius kneeled at the top of the bed, his body facing hers, and he carefully straddled her head with his knees. He reached over her and continued once again to caress her breasts, running his thumbs over the hardened surfaces of her nipples. The man knew what buttons to push to drive her wild.

Johann had removed his pants and now was positioning himself by her feet. He urged her legs open and settled between them. She was aware of how her cunt opened before him, its wet, pink surface enticing him to delve within its depths.

"You're beautiful, Kira," Johann said, appreciation echoing in his voice. "I love seeing you like this, completely abandoned, control given over to me." With that, Johann ran a finger through her folds. She felt the movement radiate through her body and regretted the moment he pulled back his hand from her dripping cunt. "I wish to see your lovely ass in the air, beckoning to me to fuck you."

Lucius released her breasts and she missed their loving touch. He assisted her in turning over and she prayed the building tension within her found release soon.

She reclined on her stomach, but Johann grasped her hips and nudged them upward. "Onto your knees so I can best see your pussy weeping for me."

Her ass in the air right in front of her mate's face, she couldn't help the surge of excitement that flowed through her veins. Her heart beat wildly and, at the sight before her, her mouth began to water—there, within an inch or two of her face, was Lucius' majestic cock.

It was hard and full. It had all the attributes a cock should have—length and width. When a bead of moisture emerged upon its purplish head, she wanted to lick it away in the hope that more would follow.

"Do you wish to suck my cock, sweet Kira?" Lucius asked huskily.

"Very much," she croaked, her tongue anxious to dart over his flesh again and again.

Then Johann ran his thumb through her juices, coating it liberally in her cream. Without a word, he began to caress her anus.

"Lick my cock, Kira. Show me the hunger you feel," Lucius urged while she reeled from the sensation of Johann touching her puckered rear entrance.

Her tongue darted out and tasted the salty essence from Lucius' cock. *Delicious.* She needed more.

And God, what a rush, with Johann playing with her like he was. He teased her sensitive anus while dipping into her cunt again and again with his fingers. First he surged one into her channel, then two. The suction was blissful and she mimicked it upon Lucius' cock.

The vampire had lost control. *He* was the one surrendering to *her* command, moaning as she sucked, savoring the taste, relishing the knowledge of this powerful vampire's desire for her. In turn, she found pleasure giving this gift to him.

As she toyed with Lucius, Johann began doing the same to her. At the feel of his tongue upon her anus, she cried out despite the cock within her mouth.

More. More. More.

Her hips bucked as he continued his savory seduction. She began to climb the heights of ecstasy with each pass of his mouth upon her.

She nearly screamed when he stopped, but then he quickly positioned his pelvis behind her, his cock head poised just outside her slit. With a finger pressed gently upon her sphincter, he entered her.

Her walls stretched, a glorious sensation of completion washing over her as she edged toward her climax. And as Johann began to pump into her channel, Lucius rotated his hips, urging her attention upon his cock. Two cocks at once. She was filled to the brink with vampire sex appeal, and they both wanted her.

Power overcame her as her orgasm crashed into her senses. Spasms racked her body, one leading into another, and another.

Johann moved faster in beat to her contractions, building to his own release. And when it came, she was elated with the power to bring her mate such shattering pleasure.

Just as Johann screamed out his climax, Lucius grunted in his own release. Warm semen sprayed into her mouth and down her throat, and she fought to take in every drop. Conscious thought was nonexistent as the three came in unison.

Kira thought every drop of strength was sucked from her body through her climax. She collapsed upon the bed in sheer exhaustion.

Lucius and Johann lay down on the bed, one on each side of her. Lucius laid a hand upon her abdomen, his touch warm and tender, and Johann covered one of her breasts with a hand.

"I love you," Johann whispered.

She sighed in contentment, feeling complete satisfaction. "I love you too."

Lucius lay silent, but Kira sensed his inner turmoil. Was he a lonely soul? She felt connected to him after he'd shown her such pleasure, but nothing like the deep bond she felt with Johann.

And she wanted to make that bond eternal, unbreakable.

Then Lucius broke the silence that had fallen over the room. "Bond before me. Let me bear witness as you two become one," he said as he rose from the bed and crouched to their side to preside over the union like a priest.

Johann faced Kira and reached for her, clasping her hand in his. The fire that burned in his blue eyes was undeniable. She felt engulfed by the sheer heat radiating from them, penetrating deep into her being.

"And now, we shall complete our destiny and become one. None will doubt our bond after tonight," Johann said.

He lifted her hand to his lips as his mind brushed against hers, reassuring and caring.

Her breathing quickened as she became more aware of her thirst for his blood. It pumped through his veins, urging her to taste its tangy essence, and she unconsciously licked her lips. He moaned as he drew her closer to him and she inhaled his masculine scent of spice and sex. The smell of their exploration still clung to his body—sweat and sexual fluids. Combined with his natural scent, it was an intoxicating mixture.

"Johann," she whispered as he brought her wrist to his lips. At that moment, no one else existed. It was only the two of them. She was unaware of Lucius looking on as she and Johann proved their loyalty and devotion.

"I take you into my body, Kira, and pledge my soul and heart to you alone. For the rest of eternity, I will be your mate, your immortal lover." Then a sharp pain pinched the inside of her wrist as he sank his fangs into her flesh.

She nearly had an orgasm from the sensation alone.

He soothed over the wound with his tongue and the holes closed before her eyes, just as any wound to her body had done for centuries.

It was time for her to drink from him. He enclosed her in his arms and her silky skin became taut with the awareness of his closeness. His bare torso was well muscled and smooth with erect nipples surrounded by tanned areolas. His skin was very pale, but it suited him. His long blond hair fell down his back in silken waves that she longed to study at length with her fingers. Her cunt reacted to this perfect specimen of a vampire, and she longed for his cock to pound into her again.

"Soon," he caressed in her mind.

"I hereby take you as my mate, my immortal lover. You shall reign beside me for the centuries to come as my equal. I give you my heart, my body and my soul." She leaned closer and her lips touched the warm pulse at his neck, then she bit into his vein.

An explosion of sweet blood and powerful emotions flooded her body and mind. With each gulp of his life elixir, she felt her entire being bond with him. In a matter of hours this strange, handsome man had become the one to hold her heart. As she drank, her soul recognized him as her missing half, the one she longed for all these centuries. Never again would she pine for love, for Johann was the only one who could truly answer her every desire for passion and caring. She was in love with this vampire who was destined to rule by her side and dominate her body in the darkness of midnight.

He wrapped her in the protection of his arms as she drank and she hated to break away, wanting to continue to take him into her. But she didn't want to drain him completely.

She drew her tongue across the wounds and they healed in a moment. He nuzzled her neck and murmured low, "Kira, I love you."

"Johann, I can barely explain it, but I love you too. I can't imagine the centuries without you."

"When I heard I was destined to be your life-mate, I wasn't happy about it. I didn't want to leave my home to come to Paris. This place held such painful memories."

"I'm glad you did come."

"But I never thought I would feel this way. I wanted to have a life-mate, but I didn't expect I would fall so hopelessly in love with you."

"Life-mates are more than physical partners. They are the second half to one's soul."

"And that's how I feel about you," Johann replied, caressing her cheek with his finger. "You're a part of me, and I could never be without you."

She was silent for a moment then asked, "Do you miss your home in the Northlands so much?"

He nodded. "I love it there." He paused then added, "But I wouldn't want to go back without you."

"Perhaps we can split our time between Paris and the Northlands."

Smiling, he proclaimed, "I think I may love you more just for that."

They kissed deeply. Kira was swept away by the emotions bombarding her heart. Yes, they would make this work. Love would see them through anything.

Lucius had slipped from the bedroom unnoticed during the blood exchange. Before Kira noticed his absence she was beneath Johann once again, his cock pushing into her slowly, drawing out the sensation, filling her at a languid pace. When she came, he joined her in her climax, bonding their bodies in the physical language of love.

As she lay with Johann nestled deep within her, Kira could feel the deep love from her mate. She felt completely content with him by her side—and cherished.

Within her mind, her lover confirmed, *"I will cherish you for all eternity, my love."*

Epilogue

Lucius left the Parisian underground and headed out into the dark streets. Johann had found an exceptional mate and part of him was jealous. Lucius never really gave the life-mate search much thought since the day he lost his one-time love, Shannon, to his maker. It seemed he was destined to remain alone. True, Lucius tried to seduce the vampiress into choosing him, but in the end, love conquered all.

Love. It existed for everyone else, but not him.

As he glided through the night, Lucius contemplated his future. Then he sensed another powerful vampire near the Eiffel Tower. It was a presence he'd not felt in many years. Strength wrapped in pain and sadness struck Lucius to the core, causing him to seek out the one who mourned in the night for his loss.

"Diablo."

Lucius transformed into a gray owl and soured upward into the air. Form hardly had purpose when a vampire was so ancient and strong. He could have dissolved into a mist and drifted upon the wind, but he preferred the solid form of a creature.

"You had her with Johann," the large dark figure said as he crouched on a steel beam near the top of the tower.

"Yes."

"I loved her once." Diablo turned his head, his blue eyes piercing Lucius.

Diablo was as powerful as Lucius, and the latter held respect for the Spanish vampire, even if he had an evil past.

Lucius was hardly any better, at one time preferring to drain his victims for the life force rush of strength.

"She was destined for Johann, not you." Lucius moved closer.

Diablo sighed. "It doesn't make it any easier for me to watch her mate with another."

Lucius understood Diablo's pain. He'd felt it when he had to leave Una behind centuries ago, when he had been forced to turn from the light to become a creature of death. Then again when he lost Shannon to Rourke. Love had never led him to anything but painful loss. But he'd seen the joy of others with their mate…a joy he helped his brother to realize.

Guilt edged about him as he watched the dark vampire mourn. Lucius had aided in the joining of Kira and his brother. He'd planted a vision of her beauty into Johann's dreams, by means of his blood-link. What else would have prompted Johann to leave his precious sanctum in the Northlands if not persuaded by steamy sex and a pair of perfect breasts? He knew his brother too well. Lucius' appearance here tonight was no coincidence.

The moment he'd spotted Kira years ago, Lucius knew her destiny lay with Johann. It was a feeling Lucius felt obligated to heed and help along. True, he'd been tempted by her beauty, but any sacrifice and effort on his part was worth it to see Johann happy—and in love.

Focusing his attention back on Diablo, Lucius mused, "Perhaps it is time for a change of scenery, my friend."

"Have somewhere in mind?"

"New Orleans. 'Tis said the city caters to our kind."

Diablo smiled, a devilish glint returning to his eyes. "Sounds perfect, my friend. Let us go to New Orleans, and drink our fill of its delights."

DESCENDANTS OF DARKNESS

Trademarks Acknowledgement

The author acknowledges the trademarked status and trademark owners of the following wordmarks mentioned in this work of fiction:

Dumpster: Dempster Systems Inc.

Chapter One
Alonso

New Orleans is North America's most haunted city. It is natural for the creatures of the night to seek refuge there amid ghost-laden cemeteries, voodoo rituals and other paranormal phenomena. Each night, they gather together in a small establishment deep in the city, hidden from human knowledge. The place is called Devil's Talon and it caters to those with special needs. There, those who are viewed as strange or bizarre are the norm.

One of the patrons is Alonso Santori, an ancient vampire of six-hundred-fifty-five years. Made during the height of the Black Death as it rolled through Europe, killing millions of people, Alonso was created and lived on as an immortal vampire. Visiting London with relatives, he was there when the plague arrived. He thought he'd avoided it, having left his home in Italy when reports of its appearance surfaced there. He should have known he couldn't outrun flea-infested rats.

So the plague came and he feared for his life. One by one, his family died before his eyes, including his sweet Vanessa.

Oh, Vanessa. How he loved her serene voice and beautiful face. He stood by helplessly as the disease ripped through her body. She'd vomited blood and her glands swelled and turned black. All he could do was watch and wait for her last breath. Once she died, he had no wish to live further. But life has a sick sense of humor.

While out at a local pub, drowning his sorrows in pints of thick ale, he met the one who would forever alter his life.

The vampire Lucius.

Lucius was the devil incarnate. He fed Alonso more alcohol and listened to his ramblings of lost love. Even now Alonso remembered the cold, ice-blue stare of those eyes. His height of more than six feet only added to his menacing air. His long white hair, unbound and falling about his shoulders, gave him an eerie sense of the spectacular and secret. Later, Alonso would learn firsthand what secrets the man held.

After he was quite inebriated, Alonso stumbled into the night with his newfound friend, looking for women to ease their carnal desires. Two red-haired ladies of the night fit the bill, and Lucius rented a room for them all. There, debauchery took on a whole new meaning.

They roughly fucked those women, but Alonso didn't care. Only visions of Vanessa danced across his mind. His one love, lost to him forever. Death robbed him of the one woman who had shown him happiness. Her deep blue eyes reflected the love for him within her heart. Love was an emotion lost to him the day she died, never to be seen or felt again.

He took the whore, beating his cock deep within her body, but passion did not drive him to spill his seed. Rage and disappointment fed the force driving him onward. He had nothing to live for anymore. Vanessa was everything.

As the woman moaned in ecstasy at his prowess, he envisioned Vanessa beneath him. His tempo slowed, and the blood boiling for revenge within his veins ebbed.

He had been betrothed to Vanessa since he was ten years old. Their marriage was arranged by their fathers, men who made a living producing and selling wine from grapes grown in Northern Italy. Alonso's father grew some of the sweetest grapes, and Vanessa's father kept the stock moving within London society. Alonso met Vanessa for the first time when he was fifteen and on a visit to London. It was love at first sight.

The whore screamed as she came beneath him, and he snapped back to reality. This wasn't his golden Vanessa. She was gone. Death stole her, cheating him of a lifetime of marital bliss.

He came violently as the whore's vaginal walls sucked his cock deeper. But it was an empty sensation. He was drained of the will to live. What was the sense of going on?

Afterward, he lay exhausted upon the vast bed, unable to move due to the booze and emotional strain.

Right next to him in the bed, Lucius continued to enjoy one of the women. He was on top of her, bent over her neck, while the other woman approached him from behind, moaning as she rubbed her naked body against his. It was most certainly erotic, but something rang sinister...evil...about the act. The woman beneath Lucius stopped moving, her eyes turned glassy and her skin lost its pink hue.

Lucius raised his head, and Alonso saw the trail of red from his lips. "Has life lost the allure for you, my friend? Do you think death would answer what you seek?" His voice was husky, and a chill crossed over Alonso's skin.

"Vanessa is gone," he said to the white-haired demon, the whore beneath him still not moving. She was *too* still.

"Death is only the beginning."

"Death is the end. Nothing is beyond death," Alonso reasoned.

Lucius chuckled. "Not necessarily so."

Alonso then realized the true nature of this man. He was unnatural, inhuman—a *demoni.* And the woman lying next to him was dead.

"Would you like to join me as my companion?" Lucius asked with an evil grin, his voice edged with vicious glee.

The girl behind him moaned again. Lucius turned, and both he and Alonso saw the whore's fingers playing at her cleft. She was deep into her own passion, unaware of the talons of danger that flitted about the room.

In a flash, Lucius tucked her body between Alonso and the dead girl. She screamed in laughter, obviously thinking it rough sex play. Then Lucius lowered his mouth just above her breast and bit down.

Alonso saw Lucius' fangs sink into her willing flesh. She gasped in pain. Fascinated, Alonso couldn't tear his gaze away as the vampire drank her blood, revitalizing his body.

She stilled, her mouth opened in a last silent plea, and her life ended. Just like that, it was over.

Alonso was certain he'd be next. This wasn't a dream. He was within the power of a vampire.

Lucius lifted his head and licked his bloodstained lips. "Ah, my friend, there is nothing like a woman's blood to make a man feel alive."

Alonso sputtered, "How could you?"

Lucius leaned back and pushed the corpses to the floor. They landed with resounding thuds. The vampire laughed, his teeth still red from his meal. Completely unaffected by his own nakedness, he flopped down next to Alonso, who stared in amazement. "I've been doing this for a long time, my friend."

"How long?"

"I was made when Vikings were the force of power over the seas."

"But weren't the Vikings a bunch of pillagers and rapists?"

The man lunged at him, pinning him down with supernatural strength. "The Norsemen were the true settlers of the world. Places you know of today wouldn't have existed without my people."

"I'm sorry," Alonso rasped, his limbs trembling in fear.

The vampire eased his hold and backed away, pushing his white hair out of his face. "I'll forgive you." He paused a moment. "I've been looking for a companion. I believe you will do nicely."

Alonso knew in his heart he had no real choice. If he said no, he would surely die as the women had, having been a witness to the ordeal. It was not how he envisioned ending it all. Even though he talked of his desire to die, he suddenly had a strong will to live.

"What if I wish to just die and not become a vampire?"

This was met with a laugh, cold and unbelieving. "I hold magic. I can sense your feelings. Your heartbeat betrays you. Living as a creature of the night has many advantages."

"Yet you seek a companion," Alonso mused aloud.

"Unfortunately, my last companion decided to go to ground. He has been resting for a hundred years. I grow impatient."

"And you mean to replace him with me?" he asked, unsure if there was any way to avoid the obvious outcome.

"Companions are fairly temporary for vampires. The partnership lasts for a few hundred years then it dissolves. It is our way."

"Why not find a woman?"

The vampire shot from the bed. His powerful body was perfection in the dim light of the lamp. Shadows sculpted about Lucius' body in a dark caress. "Women… There was only one woman I wished to bestow the Demon's Kiss upon, but she was the life-mate of another—my maker." The vampire paused his agitated pacing and turned to Alonso still lying on the bed. "I want my companion to be a comrade, a partner in the hunt. You have the kind of dark looks that appeal to women. Together, we can hunt about the world and feast upon humans ready for the taking as simply as a flick of the wrist."

He wanted Alonso to help prey upon humans, just like he had unwittingly done that night. "What if I say no?"

"Then you will die a most horrible death. I will make you as I, but I will leave the sun to finish you off. It is a most unpleasant experience, or so I've been told."

This vampire had him by the balls, and there was only one real choice to make.

Now, years later, Alonso shook his head to clear away the horrid images of that long ago night, which seemed to have happened only yesterday.

They had traveled about Italy, France, Spain and England, feeding upon the living, mainly women seduced into a night of sex. Their victims ranged from all classes of society—rich and poor. Alonso had a hard time dealing with the death of any human. A hundred years rolled by, and he had grown unsettled. Lucius had begun taking more risks—he had loved the daring prowl of hunting the loved ones of those who hunted their kind. The greater the danger, the greater the thrill.

Years passed and Alonso became disenchanted with the lifestyle. He tried to sip from several humans each night, not killing to feed. It became more acceptable within his soul to exist without taking a life. In turn, he and Lucius fought over the method and separated ways while on a visit in Italy. Alonso took the opportunity to rest at his family's winery, now in the hands of relatives he'd never met. He kept his presence unknown, out of sight from them as he watched from afar. It was a lonely existence, but he had gone through so much.

Worst of it, Lucius was still out there, feeding off the living. His powers were great, increasing with each century. It was a wonder Lucius made it through those tough years when vampire hunting had been the rage. That was part of the reason Alonso eventually came to America, to the Big Easy. Others of his kind surrounded the city, making him feel not quite so alone and isolated.

It was true, vampires were solitary creatures as a whole, but some did travel together in a coven, or met nightly as they did at the Devil's Talon. Sometimes there was safety in numbers, and there were more vampires than any human realized in New Orleans. Popular fiction touched on the legends, hinting at the life beyond the night shadows, but only those who lived it knew the whole story.

Turning down a dark, forbidding alley off Canal Street, Alonso made his way to the hidden entrance of the exclusive club. Invisible to human eyes due to a simple protection spell, the club was visible only to vampires and other supernatural creatures.

Various scraps of paper and cans littered the alley, and moisture from an early evening shower rose in a mist from the heated street surface. Alonso heard the clicking of his boots against the cobblestones as well as the scurrying of rodents and their tiny hearts rapidly beating. They were sounds he had learned to live with.

The overwhelming bombardment of noises was the hardest thing for him to get used to after being turned. Some would think it was drinking blood that required the most adjustment. No, it was the thousands of sounds unheard by the human ear. Roaches crawling along the insides of walls, rats gnawing at their fleas and—the most disturbing—blood flowing with each pump of the heart in every living creature were all among the racket Alonso had to filter through his mind. Heightened senses were a curse at times.

Stopping before the large black door, Alonso felt the protective spell. Reaching through with his mind, he called to the doorman, who answered by opening a small peephole. Wood slid back across the hole and the door opened, the spell dropping away to allow his entry.

"*Ciao*, Jack," Alonso said as he passed the burly doorman.

"Nice to see you tonight, Mr. Santori." Jack closed the door, replacing the spell.

"Genevieve here tonight?"

"No, Mr. Santori. She's off traveling to Los Angeles and New York City. She's looking into starting clubs there."

Genevieve St. Claire, the daughter of a slave owner who was turned during the dark years before the Civil War, was the woman responsible for the club that catered to vampires and other creatures of the night. The Devil's Talon had an international reputation and she was apparently expanding.

Alonso stepped into the club, alive with activity. Techno-beat music pumped through loudspeakers. He was surprised the walls didn't shake on his way in. Obviously the spell also kept the music from giving away the location.

Red, green and blue lights flashed and waved through the crowd, dancing in tempo with the powerful beats. Vampires of all shapes, sizes, colors and backgrounds converged on the club, and many lavished in the freedom to have fun.

"Alonso, honey, long time, no see." Monique, a Creole female turned a mere two hundred years ago, pressed up against him. Her luscious curves were tempting, and her cappuccino-colored skin exotic. Match that with her sultry voice and accent—and an eagerness to please sexually—and it was hard to resist her offers of passionate nights.

"Mon, you're *magnifica,*" he said, planting a kiss on her forehead. He liked rolling in the sheets with her on occasion, but tonight he wasn't in the mood for unemotional sex. He felt somewhat melancholy every year on this night—the anniversary of his turning.

"Mmm, Alonso—I'd ask to screw you, but I sense your mood."

"Maybe some other time, Mon."

"You bet. Hey, want to join us? Both Leo and Titania are here."

"Sure." He followed her to a table located along the farthest wall from the dance floor.

Titania was a strawberry-blonde vampiress from Ireland who came to America during the Potato Famine back in the mid-1800s. A rogue vampire had turned her one night on the streets of New York City. It was probably for the best, as the workhouse in which she had toiled was killing her. Living in an overcrowded tenement, close to starvation and a victim of a textile company using its workers' desperation as a weapon to force more hours upon them, Titania was on the path to death before she met the vampire.

Now, she sat talking with Leo, another vampire of Italian descent, made during the Italian Renaissance. He often bragged he was an apprentice to the great Michelangelo, but he never could prove it by his drawings. Leo was tall, dark and handsome in a Mediterranean kind of way, and women naturally flocked to him. He could pick and choose from where his meals came.

"Hey, Alonso," he said, looking up to him with dark eyes.

"*Ciao*, Leo…Ti."

Leo took a sip of his drink, a glass of deep red, fresh blood, the house specialty. "Raife will be here in a bit," he added as Alonso took a seat.

Raife was the British addition to their group, made in the time when Elizabeth ruled as a "king in skirts". He was one of her privateers who fought Philip the First's Spanish Armada, and he always had wonderful tales of adventure to share. It was his way of returning to the time when he was human and happy to be alive. Nowadays, he had almost lost the purpose of his vampire existence. Somewhere along the way he had lost hope of finding a life-mate.

They all longed for a life-mate. Hundreds of years of craving tended to make a vampire cranky from time to time. Many lost optimism of ever finding the mate to their heart, and embraced the darker side of their existence. They became like Lucius—*demoni scuri*, dark demons, as Alonso referred to them. They were of a different mindset, practically a different breed of vampire. They were Satan's spawn, spreading death and fear in their wake.

"Alonso, you look as if you're a million miles away." Monique placed a hand on his shoulder, slightly shaking him.

"*Dolente*, sorry, *mia amica*. This night is always troublesome for me. It's like this every year."

"Ah, *oui,* the anniversary," Mon said, then took a sip of her Bloody Mary. The drink took on a whole new meaning at Devil's Talon. It was a mixture of donated blood from various humans, primarily those who volunteered their services to the vampires.

"Wonder whatever happened to Lucius," Leo mused. "He seems to have just disappeared."

"He's out there somewhere. I can feel him." Unfortunately, Alonso sensed the *demoni* was way too close for comfort.

* * * * *

Jolie shuffled the cards as she watched the crowd of bar patrons that were mainly tourists. She made a good bit of money during tourist season. Of course, Mardi Gras was prime time for readings. She could easily make a few grand during the celebration.

People visited the city for its rich history and magical mysteries, like the Voodoo Queen Marie Laveau. Even today, more than a hundred years after her death, people visited the Voodoo Queen's tomb, asking for help in finding love and other requests.

Jolie had also gone there this morning to make her wish. She had visited the tomb several years before out of curiosity but had never appealed to the Queen's spirit for anything. Today, something drove Jolie to ask for assistance in her love life. Finding a good man had turned into a sort of obsession.

Today was her thirtieth birthday, and things looked a bit grim. She had done numerous Tarot readings for herself and they all ended the same—inconclusive. It was as though the cards wanted to hide her future mate. Desperate times called for desperate measures, so she had visited the Voodoo Queen.

Standing before the tomb, Jolie had gazed upon the marks left behind by others wishing for happiness and answers to their problems. At thirty, what was her problem? What drove her here to the Voodoo Queen?

One word—loneliness. She had thus far been unable to find the man who could meet her mind and touch her heart. In thirty years, she'd had affairs, but nothing deeper than a few nights of pleasure. None had shown her the fulfillment of love. She wasn't growing desperate to find that one heart-match. She was losing hope. Perhaps a plea to the Queen, as remotely possible as it may be, could help.

She believed in magic completely, which was why she took the trip to the cemetery. She made her livelihood reading Tarot and knew the cards never lied. Psychic gifts were a part of her life, ever since she could remember. Even as a child, her mother swore Jolie was special.

When she was about four, she had a pet pony. Jolie loved the pony like anyone would love a pet dog or cat. This pony, Peanuts, thought he was a dog—at least he acted like one. They were buddies and had played every day.

Then one night, Jolie had sensed something very wrong. She cried and screamed the night through, driving her mother to the verge of tears. The next morning, they found Peanuts dead, hit by a truck in the street. Apparently, he had gotten out of his pen during the night. Even as a child, Jolie had known it was the pony's love for her that had driven him to seek her out. She had sensed the impending danger that caused her such turmoil that night.

Since then, Jolie had become more aware of her sixth sense. No, the dead didn't talk to her, but she could sense things before they happened. Naturally, Tarot card reading came easily to her.

She continued to shuffle, concentrating on the cards, shutting out the murmurs and music around her. Her booth within the Razzoo—a popular Bourbon Street pick-up bar—was in the back, out of the way, yet gave her a view of the entire room.

Then she saw him.

"Predatory" came to mind. Evil. Tall, with long white-blonde hair and piercing blue eyes, he was unlike any other man she had ever seen. Her inner voice told her to be wary.

Dressed all in black, he carried a walking stick topped with a silver cast of—good Lord—a wolf. A foreboding chill crawled down her spine.

He stopped before the booth, glancing at her tabletop sign before looking at her. "Good evening, Madam Jolie."

His voice sounded odd, as if his British accent was put on. Why would he act the part of an English nobleman? He looked like a Viking—huge, blonde and sinfully gorgeous.

"Sir." She nodded and held out her hand in welcome. "Pleased to meet you."

"No, the pleasure is all mine," he said with a smile, taking her hand in his.

Heat pulsed through his fingers into her own, shooting up her arm.

He pulled out the chair across from her and sat. "I wish for you to read my fortune in the cards."

She peered at his face, the realization of darkness within his soul overpowering her. Yet, he intrigued her. What was it about him that was so...different? He had his own magic about him, radiating in his sinister aura.

"I'm afraid you probably could tell me more than I could tell you."

His thumb brushed the back of her hand in sensual circles. "Nonsense. Please, I wish to see if love will ever enter my life."

She pulled her hand away and instantly missed his touch. He was way too dangerous, but still she found him desirable. She shuffled the cards and concentrated on the reading, trying to blank out her reaction to his closeness. Laying the cards on the table, she instructed him to cut the deck into three piles.

After gathering them up, she laid out the cards in a traditional Celtic cross spread.

Her body shook while she absorbed the meaning of the cards laid out before her. He was truly an evil soul—searching for meaning, a purpose to continue.

"Tell me, dear lady," his hypnotic voice washed over her, causing her skin to tingle. "Will I ever find my true love?"

Reading the cards, she nodded. "The woman of your heart is close, though you've waited a long time for her to appear. The Empress is the woman you seek. And you should meet her soon, but be patient."

He snorted a laugh. "Patient? I've waited hundreds of years to find my queen, and you ask me to be patient?"

What did he mean by "hundreds of years"? "I'm sorry, but at least your heart's desire is coming."

He reached across the table to cup her cheek. Her entire body reacted to his touch, inflaming her. No, she mustn't let him gain control. Her inner voice screamed caution. Giving in to the baser bodily desire would mean death at the hands of this strange man.

"Look into my eyes, sweet Jolie. Tell me—can you satisfy a man's yearning to be loved for this one night?"

Her eyes drifted closed, relishing the tender touch of his hand on her face. All she could do was whisper a plea within her mind. *Help me.*

Chapter Two

Help me.

Alonso heard it in the recesses of his mind. A remote connection to a woman in need. He focused on the voice and zeroed in on her surroundings.

Humans. Music. Alcohol. And…

Lucius. The bastard had indeed returned.

"Sorry, I have to go," Alonso said, jumping up from the table.

"What is it?" Leo asked.

"Lucius. He's here. Close. And a woman is calling to me." *How could that be,* he wondered. *Did she have some special power?*

"I'm coming along," Leo said, rising.

"Let me face him myself. I know him more than anyone. If I need help, I'll call."

Alonso raced out of the club, leaving behind his friends and the pounding music. In the alley, he began to transform. His body shifted, changing size and shape, into a golden eagle. With a flap of his grand wings, he lifted into the air, homing in on Lucius.

He had a blood bond to the *demoni* and could sense everything Lucius felt. He could use that connection to find the vampire in the vast city. Soaring above the historic buildings that lined the streets of New Orleans, he closed in on his maker. He was on Bourbon Street in a human dance club, deep in the heart of the French Quarter. Alonso traveled as fast as the wind to head off the imminent danger.

There was something to be said of a strange woman calling to him. And why was he able to hear her and sense her surroundings? He hoped he had the chance to find out before Lucius made her his next meal. Never had he heard a human call to him without some sort of blood bond. This woman was indeed unique.

Bourbon Street was alive with nightlife activity. It was the perfect place for a vampire to seek out a meal. At least, for a vampire wanting to take a life with his meal.

Only the *demoni scuri*, like Lucius, murdered for their meals. Once vampires killed, they became more distant and isolated. Crossing one of them was always dangerous. Many were largely independent, but some took on companions, partners in the hunt. Lucius went through stages of wanting a companion. Alonso hoped he didn't have to cross another *demoni scuri* in his search. Lucius was deadly enough.

Below, within the Razzoo, he felt Lucius. He hadn't gotten the girl outside yet. Alonso wasn't too late. He landed in a dark shadow cast from one of the nearby buildings and shifted back to his human form.

Inside the crowded club, the smells of sweat, perfumes, body odor and alcohol assaulted him. Hundreds of human hearts beat wildly to the rock music pumping through huge amplifiers. Sexual excitement laced the air as men and woman flirted and made their choices for the night in an attempt to satisfy their primal needs.

Making his way through the crowd, several women threw themselves against him, rubbing their bodies against his. If he hadn't been there to confront Lucius, he may have taken them to a dark recess for a few sips of their delectable life fluid.

In the corner, he spotted Lucius' long white hair. Carefully, Alonso approached the table where Lucius held a woman's hand.

She looked up and her gaze locked with Alonso's.

He felt as if the air had been sucked out of the room. Those eyes, so dark and lovely, pleaded with him. Her creamy complexion was perfection, and her dark raven-black hair was swept up into a mass of elaborate curls and waves. She wore a velvet shawl of black, with swirls of jewel-tone reds. She looked like a palm reader or…

A psychic? Could that be why he had heard her call? But why him?

"Ah, Alonso," Lucius said without turning. "How nice of you to come, my old friend and companion. Sit and meet the lovely Jolie. She was just reading my fortune as told by the cards."

"I don't think so."

Lucius gazed up at Alonso. The intense, cool-blue calculation in the vampire's eyes struck him. Lucius wanted her for more than a night's meal. He wanted to mate with her.

Alonso swore then he wouldn't allow anyone to have her. He wanted her for himself.

He extended a hand toward the woman. "Come with me, now."

"Careful, Alonso. I saw her first."

"But you won't have her."

* * * * *

Lucius rose from his seat and stood eye to eye with Alonso. Both being of great height, they looked like a pair of warriors about to battle. Jolie needed to get the hell out of Dodge before it was decided who would get the spoils of their battle—her. She was not about to give in to either of their macho antics, even though the dark-haired newcomer seemed familiar—as though he had walked out of one of her dreams. An erotic dream, that is.

Not only was the one called Alonso tall and handsome, he had gorgeous, long, straight black hair and a solid-looking body. He wore black dress pants and a white oxford shirt, open partly down his chest, giving her a nice view of golden skin covering toned sinew. He could be Aries, the war god, from the way he stood, matching height and strength with the Thor-like Lucius.

Not wanting to stick around for the outcome, she gathered her cards and shoved them into her bag, along with her table cover and candles. No time for neatness. She slipped out of the booth and edged away from the men, now talking in hushed tones. Probably whispered threats, judging by the way they sized up each other.

Odd how this stranger had showed up only minutes after she sensed herself in deep trouble. Unable to see how she could break free of the menacing danger lurking beneath Lucius' smile, she had pleaded within her mind for help. She never figured anyone would come to her aid.

Was it coincidence or had he heard her?

No one had ever had that kind of connection to her.

Jolie got to the club doors and left, unwilling to look back in case they realized she had gone. Out on Bourbon Street, she blended in with the night crowd of club patrons.

She hailed a cab. Once inside, she fell back onto the vinyl seat and breathed a sigh of relief. At least she got out of that one.

Thinking back, she wondered about the dark man. Looking at him, her secret fantasies had popped to life. She was sure she had seen him before in a vision but had only passed it off as fantasy. He was definitely reality. A man didn't have the right to look so sinfully sexy. One look from those dark eyes and her body had quivered with excitement. Her heart skipped a beat and her breathing had become labored. Even the juncture of her thighs had moistened at the sight of him. She had ached for his touch the moment she saw him. It was criminal to be so instantly attracted to a man.

About ten minutes later, the cab drove up to her apartment building on St. Charles and she got out. After climbing the stairs, she made it inside her small apartment.

Decorated in mystic jewel tones, it was her comfort zone. Here, she felt safe and secure.

But was she really?

Those men looked beyond dangerous. Actually, meeting up with the large Italian one would be a pleasure. Hell, she'd be up for a night of rumpy-bumpy with him anytime.

* * * * *

"She's gone."

Lucius smirked. "I know. I sensed her slip away. No matter. I will find her again."

"Stay away from her," Alonso growled.

"Why? You staking claim to her?"

"Yes."

Lucius chuckled, a deep, ominous sound. "Really, Alonso? Do you think after all this time you've finally found your mate?"

Alonso couldn't explain it. He had felt it the instant he saw her. There was a connection, an unexplainable link between them. Just thinking of her delicate beauty made him hard with want. The urge to seek her out in the night to bind himself to her body grew overwhelming. Letting her leave the club had been torture, but he knew it had been for the best. She needed to escape Lucius' intents, if only temporarily until Alonso could properly protect her. He'd find her with their mental connection once again.

Since when had he ever taken to any female so quickly? Her dark beauty had mesmerized him at one glance. On the spot, he recognized her as his life-mate. He couldn't let Lucius near her.

"I claim her. That's enough for you to leave her be. Don't come near her, Lucius," he said with a snarl.

Lucius sat again at the table, casually examining the silver tip of his walking stick. "It's getting harder and harder for me to face each night. Somehow, I know something is out there waiting for me. Hunting me."

"With all the evil you've done over the centuries, I'm not surprised something hunts you."

Lucius looked up and smiled. It was not comforting in any way. He had devious plans going on in that twisted mind. "Go find her, my friend. If she is not marked by you by tomorrow night, I will proceed to make her my own."

"I'd kill you first."

"Then go to her now."

As Alonso left Razzoo, he wondered why Lucius allowed him first chance with the woman.

Sniffing the air, he picked up her faint scent of vanilla musk and woman. God, he ached for her.

Would she let a complete stranger into her life? He had to at least see her again and talk to her. Only then could he know if she was the one.

His life-mate. Could it be, after all these centuries, he had finally found her?

Ducking into the shadows, out of view of the drunken partiers, he changed once again into his alternate form. The golden eagle leapt into the air and soared over the Big Easy.

No wonder it was called thus. Humans and vampires alike found partners for whatever their fancy, be it a blood meal or sexual gratification. And at the moment, Alonso wanted both. And only the woman, Jolie, would do.

At St. Charles Street he sensed her nearness. From an apartment building, the scent grew stronger. She was inside. Flying on the night wind, he circled the building, zeroing in on her apartment. On the second floor, a light went on. He saw her through the window, brushing her hair, silhouetted by white frilly curtains.

After landing, he shifted back to his human form. Her scent permeated his nostrils, driving him insane with need. He longed to see her, touch her. The short glimpse of her at the club had not been enough.

He picked up a few pebbles from the street, lightly throwing one against the window.

Her face turned toward the sound before turning away once again, as she continued to brush her long black hair.

He tossed another, and she pulled back the curtain and gazed out. Spotting him, she opened the window. "What in the world are you doing here? How'd you find me?"

"I followed you."

It was sort of true. He had followed her scent. Her hair looked soft around her shoulders, and she wore only a thin, white cotton nightgown. He saw the dark areolas of her breasts against the thin fabric. Her nipples strained against the flimsy material.

His cock twitched. Sniffing the air once again, he could smell her excitement. She was beautiful and desirous, and he knew she wanted him too.

"What happened to Eric the Viking?" she asked with a laugh.

"Who? Oh, you mean Lucius. He's back at the club."

She seemed to consider something, and he hoped she'd invite him up. But what kind of woman would invite a total stranger into her apartment in this day and age?

"Want to come up?"

Damn—*his* woman would!

* * * * *

What the hell was she doing, inviting a strange man into her apartment? But something about him appealed to her. It wasn't just his handsome face or the broad expanse of his shoulders that made her mouth water. Something she couldn't put a name to made her want to know him more. Her body hummed to life at the sight of him, and she knew instinctively she could trust him. Perhaps it was her psychic ability that helped her determine his character. She was always a good judge of people. However, there was something more to this man and his blond counterpart. What was that sense of evil—more so in Lucius—that made her want to pause?

She hoped her instinct was right about Alonso. Or maybe it was her pussy's ache speaking to her. How long had it been since it was tended to properly? The thought of Alonso brushing her clit with his thumb was enough to make her moan. She was hot, needy, and she wanted relief. Only this man with the dark eyes could ease that powerful need.

A knock sounded at the door, and she shuddered. When she opened it, there he was—tall, dark and tempting. His long, straight black hair fell loose about his shoulders and she craved to run her fingers through its silky texture. Another jolt of sexual awareness shot through her body, ending at the apex of her thighs. Her intimate muscles contracted in animalistic recognition. The word "mate" skittered across her mind as she gazed into his dark eyes. She could easily sink into those brown depths.

"*Ciao*," he said with a warm smile. "I'm Alonso." His accent, obviously Italian, washed over her senses.

"Jolie," she offered. "Come in."

He entered the room with an air of supreme dominance. The spacious apartment seemed much smaller with his presence. She closed the door and watched him move about the room, examining the decor.

"Unusual apartment, but it suits you. I like it."

"Thanks. Make yourself at home." She stepped toward him.

He gazed at her with an intense heat in his eyes. Sex. Hot, passionate sex, the look said to her, loud and clear. Could she give herself to him for a night of lust?

Hell, yes.

"Ah, could…could I get you something to drink—coffee, a glass of wine?" she stammered as she walked to the kitchen.

"I never drink…wine," he said with a slight chuckle and a bad Hungarian accent.

She smiled. "A fan of old horror movies?"

"I find some of the films about vampires quite entertaining."

"Those are my favorites too. Bela Lugosi was an awesome Dracula, but Frank Langella was much sexier."

"I like both of them," he said, closing the distance between them, the crackle in the air utterly palpable. "Have you ever dreamed of a vampire coming to seduce you into an eternity of love and passion?"

"I think there are many women who dream of a love everlasting."

He stood so close she could smell his clean, spicy scent. Placing his palm on her hip, he pulled her to him. Her body fit perfectly, his hard planes an intoxicating contrast to her softer curves. His hypnotic gaze melted her against him further.

"Would you want me to be the vampire to give you that love?"

Could she truly do this? Her body moved against him, recognizing him as a perfect match. Her heart raced within her chest and she felt lightheaded. She wanted him. Could she risk giving herself to a stranger she just met?

"Well?" he asked, pressing her closer to his body. Heat radiated from him, the warmth wrapping about her, heightening her senses. The brush of his thigh against her cunt made her groan.

One night of passion, throwing caution to the wind, would do wonders for her. She'd been on a sexual dry spell and this hunk was seducing her into promises of ecstasy.

He nibbled at her neck and shivers skittered down her spine. How could she think clearly with him doing that?

"Don't think, Jolie. Just act," he whispered.

She encircled his neck with her arms and whispered in surrender, "Make love to me, Alonso."

Her body felt on fire. Her thin nightgown became a barrier to her would-be lover. She wanted to bare herself before him. She knew him for all of ten minutes and already she ached with need for his touch, for him to fill her body with his, bonding them together as true lovers.

"I will," he breathed against her lips before brushing them lightly in a gentle kiss.

Melding of lips in soft kisses quickly turned demanding, hungry. At the first touch of his tongue against hers, she thought she'd explode. Her hands traveled over his strong shoulders, mapping the rippling muscles beneath her palms. To bring him closer into the devouring kisses, she pulled his head down, running her fingers through the long, silky threads of his hair. God, it felt better than she'd imagined. She groaned against his mouth as their bodies rubbed together, his bulging erection brushing the sensitive apex of her thighs.

"Take me," she rasped when he broke the kiss to nibble her earlobe. Tiny shivers rose along her skin.

Alonso lifted her in his arms as though she weighed nothing. He carried her to the bedroom and eased her down upon the clean white bed sheets. He backed away a step and unbuttoned his shirt. Her hips had a life of their own as she wriggled upon the bed, aching for his touch. Once his shirt was off, her fingers itched to touch him, memorize his body, each and every inch. And she would.

Unzipping his pants, he lowered them to the floor. His shaft stood large from a thick nest of black hair. The purplish head was shining in the dim light of her bedside table lamp, and a drop of fluid dotted the tip. She licked her lips, wanting to taste the salty essence. No man had the right to look so sinful naked. But then, he was hers only for tonight.

Only tonight? She suddenly didn't want only one night. She wanted more.

She stripped away her nightgown to reveal her nakedness. He moaned as he stood beside the bed, while she traced her body with her own hands. She cupped her breasts and flicked the already taut nipples, and her hips moved in rhythm, tempting him to touch her pussy.

Her bud ached for his touch and she needed it now! She spread her legs and dipped a hand to cover the trimmed patch above her cleft. Brushing a finger over her clit, she gasped.

He crawled onto the bed between her legs. Grasping her thighs, he lowered to her nub and tentatively licked it once. She bucked and he chuckled. "Sweet Jolie, *mia amore*, don't rush. Enjoy our first time. And it is only our first of many."

"Only the first?" she gasped between breaths.

He lightly licked her once again. "We're lovers for the rest of eternity. You are mine."

Then he plunged his mouth into her cunt, devouring her, drinking the juices flowing from his touch. His tongue swirled around her clit and then dipped into her slit. She couldn't think on his words as she climbed upward to her release.

His tongue danced within her. All conscious thought fled as she writhed from her mounting pleasure. She followed his skillful command. His hands held her secure as his face delved in her pussy. She dipped her fingers to his hair, guiding him onward.

The world shattered around her in rainbows of colors. She screamed with each wave of her instant climax, and he continued to lap at her channel, his tongue filling her passage and tasting each drop of her honeyed cream.

The rolling spasms ebbed, and she lay drained of energy. She was vaguely aware of him sliding up her body and lying next to her, caressing a breast with his palm. Then slowly, her mind began to work again. Did he say she was his? Hell, she'd go for that. He'd given her the best orgasm she'd ever known in a matter of seconds. For that alone, he was a keeper. Damn, what would his cock do to her once he filled her? She'd probably pass out from the pleasure.

"Jolie, *mia amore*, are you okay?" he asked with some concern, because her eyes were still closed.

Moaning, she turned to him and nuzzled his neck. "I'm better than okay, you Italian stallion. How can I find you so desirable after knowing you for only a short while?"

"We're life-mates. I knew it the moment I saw you." He ran his hand through her hair, keeping her close.

"Life-mates?"

"My destined lover."

"I like the sound of that." She licked the salty skin of his neck and nipped him along his collarbone. He inhaled sharply at her teeth grating along his skin. "I want you inside me, Alonso." Her voice became husky and seductive when she added, "Fill me."

He pushed her onto her back and slid on top of her. His weight was not only arousing but comforting. He was the man she'd waited all her life for. The man she'd dreamed of finding. The man she thought only fantasies created.

Nudging apart her legs, he paused before her opening. The engorged head of his cock rubbed against her clit, covering him with the juices of her desire. She moaned and widened her legs, thrusting upward to take him.

He entered her in a swift stroke. She called out his name as he filled her completely. After nearly pulling out, he thrust back inside. Torture. Pleasurable pain. She needed him to move faster but didn't want to rush the exquisite feeling of him moving in and out of her.

The tempo was slow and relishing.

"God, I need to come again," she panted.

"Slow down. Enjoy this," he sad in a husky voice as he continued the torture of entering then retreating.

They bonded with each thrust, each connection. Jolie felt their bodies become one. Souls uniting. Hearts beating in unison. Minds melding together. She worshipped the incredible mating of her own self to Alonso. It was unlike any other experience in her life. She was no longer one person without him, and he the same, incomplete without her.

He licked the skin around her neck, tasting her as he moved within her channel. Above her left breast, a sharp pain pierced her, ripping through her body as an intense orgasm hit them both. Her muscles squeezed around his cock with each climactic wave, and he spilled into her. Milking him, she rode out the rapturous contractions, long and cherishing. He broke his hold on her breast and screamed with his climax.

Nothing mattered in the world other than this moment. Jolie wondered at the thousands of visions passing before her mind's eye as her body shuddered in climax. She saw nights to come within his arms, giving her body and soul to this man. But there were many other visions of a distant past, of Alonso as a child, racing through aisles of grape vines, running from his brothers in play. Alonso mourning over a blonde woman, deadly looking with blackened skin. The blond Viking biting into Alonso's neck. Alonso and Lucius seducing women into sex and feasting upon their writhing flesh. She saw the progression of his companionship with Lucius deteriorating into resentment, Alonso escaping into the night, fleeing from the…*demoni*. In this climactic moment she learned all about him. Everything.

Including his secret.

Chapter Three

Hours later, with his arms enwrapping Jolie, Alonso was sated for the first time in more than six centuries. He never thought any woman could take the place of his lost Vanessa. No, that wasn't right. Jolie didn't replace Vanessa—she opened a part of his soul previously untouched. His Vanessa was in the past. Jolie was his future. He had found his life-mate.

Could he bring her over to his existence? Could he damn her to a life as a vampire?

It wasn't that being a vampire was completely unpleasant. He didn't mind it, on the whole. The loneliness of yearning for his one life-mate had been the worst part. But now, she was bound to him. So would all eternity be so bad?

She slept soundly, but he felt the dawn approach. Slipping her out of his embrace, he loathed the break of contact. With her he was complete, all his pieces joined in perfect harmony. Leaving her before the morning light would be difficult, but he'd find her that night. At least he had marked her so Lucius couldn't have her.

Would that keep the *demoni* from trying to claim her? Tonight, he'd make sure he was with her so Lucius didn't. He didn't trust the vampire in the least. A century as his companion taught him that.

After pulling on his clothes, he leaned over her naked figure and tugged a blanket around her. Dropping a kiss on her forehead, he whispered, "Until tonight, sweet Jolie. I'll come for you."

Passing a hand over her forehead, he snatched away the painful memories of his past transferred to her during their joining. Not until she was fully ready could he let her remember such dark moments in his history.

He left the apartment and, changing into the golden eagle once more, flew away from his mate.

Within the historic St. Louis Cemetery number one was where Alonso found rest. He detested slumbering in a tomb, but it was the only way to be sure of no sunlight entering and no humans disturbing his peace. The door weighed a couple hundred pounds, and no mortal could easily lift it.

Alonso had bought the tomb under the guise of his death when he arrived in New Orleans in the 1800s. It was convenient, especially when burial underground was not the practice. New Orleans was built below sea level, so digging a grave would be likened to digging a well. It filled with water within minutes. So the Cities of the Dead sprouted up. Aboveground tombs lined the cemeteries and past residents of the city rested within them, from politicians to pirates, voodoo queens to shopkeepers.

Not to mention the hundreds of vampires using them as their resting places, like Alonso.

After opening the door to his tomb with the wave of a hand, he stepped inside and settled in for the day. Just as the sun began to peak over the horizon, he shut the door and climbed into his coffin. He fell into a peaceful sleep, dreaming of the woman who held his heart and soul within her hands. For the first time in centuries, he would rest well.

* * * * *

Jolie awoke later that morning, missing Alonso's welcoming heat next to her.

Why did he leave her alone? Men were always doing crap like that and she hated it. Wham, bam, thank you ma'am.

But then, Alonso seemed different last night. Had he spoken the truth? When they'd had sex, it seemed more than a mere physical bond—it was as though she had bonded her soul to him.

"Don't worry, sweet Jolie. We are life-mates. I will love you forever."

She heard him within her mind. Somehow it didn't spook her. After all, she had called to him the night before. He did answer her call, right?

"Yes." His dreamy deep voice resounded in her mind.

"We need to talk more next time, Alonso. I have so many questions to ask you," she said mentally to him.

"Tonight, I will answer your questions. Right now, I must rest."

Then the link was broken. Yet she still felt him in the recesses of her mind. She had always been psychic, but she had never been able to talk to someone through her thoughts. This was extraordinary. Was he psychic too, or something completely different? The vision of a vampire crept along the edges of her consciousness.

A vampire? Why, of all things, would she think that?

A vague vision crossed her mind—indistinct, like a shadow creeping in the darkness. She struggled to remember but found it difficult to focus. It was as though the memory was deleted from her mind. For the next few moments she lay there forcing herself to concentrate, but only the black form, evil yet tortured, remained in her mind.

Getting up, she threw on a robe and walked into the living room. After grabbing her bag from a nearby chair, she rummaged through it to find her Tarot. She pulled out the cards and table cover, then set up to do a reading for herself on the coffee table before the couch. She often did her own spreads but today, she knew the Tarot would reveal more than ever before. While shuffling the cards, she concentrated on Alonso and their future. After cutting them into three piles, she gathered them and cast down a Celtic spread. There, within the cards, she saw clearly the question of her heart.

Alonso was the King of Cups, which meant he was a new love, a man determined to be everything she could ask for—a loving husband.

The other cards, however, concerned her…the Tower matched with the Lovers card. Would there be trouble ahead for them from a dangerous man, portrayed by the Magician?

Then it hit her. Oh, God, it's the man from last night—Lucius!

Shaking, she stared at the Magician, evil and wanting to cause chaos. Was there some personal reason that Lucius wanted to hurt Alonso? What was the history between the men?

Old, ancient souls. They weren't mere men. She had felt something more in the air between them. Something sinister and magical…and menacing.

Trouble lay ahead involving the two men and she stood in the middle of their feud. Lucius was going to cause problems, according to the cards. And she knew he'd appear tonight. It was destiny playing out. Or maybe it was her sixth sense giving her fair warning.

If she was to meet with Lucius and Alonso, she wanted to be ready. She would mentally prepare for the confrontation—and a night that could possibly change her life forever.

* * * * *

By the time the sun went down, Bourbon Street was already abuzz with activity. Jolie passed through the crowd, clutching her bag to her chest. Dressed in her typical mystic dress and velvet shawl, she felt ready for an evening of Tarot readings. She really didn't know what to expect, though. In the air hung a sense of danger, and it seeped through her pores. Tonight her entire life would change.

At the Razzoo, a large muscled bouncer with a shaved head waved her inside. Just a look from him could deter drunks from getting out of line. Jolie wondered if he could match off with the powerful Alonso or Lucius.

After last night's passionate encounter, she at first thought her connection to Alonso was just psychic. Then she had seen the marks above her breast when she stripped for her shower. They looked like vampire bite marks. New Orleans was rumored to be a favorite haunt of the supernatural, and she believed in many of the tales of ghosts and magic, so why not vampires too? Maybe Anne Rice had it right.

So she was falling for a vampire. Okay, no normal man for her. She should have known. Her vision of a vampire that morning was confirmed when she saw the marks on her body.

Alonso the vampire. He had given her a clue last night before they made love—"Would you want me to be the vampire to give you that love?"

She had thought it was just a part he was playing because they had talked a bit about Dracula. But then, he had an aura of power, dark and mysterious, emanating from him. As he looked into her eyes, she had felt it intently. It drew her to him like a deprived woman.

Could she live with the fact her lover was a vampire? He had bitten her last night—did that mean she'd become one?

Images of them slick with sweat as their bodies slid together, perfectly matched, filled her mind. Liquid heat gathered between her thighs at the remembrance of him within her, moving in tempo with their building passion. He filled her like no other ever had, and her body hummed even now. She wanted him right now, pounding his cock into her.

"Mmm, nothing like the scent of an aroused woman," a deep masculine voice said from behind.

She turned to face the white-haired devil. "Leave me alone," she said, trying to make her way through the club.

"Oh, Jolie, you know by now what I am, along with the dark Alonso."

She approached her usual table and set down her bag. "I know," she whispered, then faced him. "Why are you following me?"

He stepped closer, towering over her. She smelled his expensive cologne, a scent intoxicating and masculine. "Because I want you for myself."

His striking blue eyes gazed intently into hers, and she felt this powerful vampire invading her mind.

He laughed low, grasping her upper arm and pulling her to him. "Don't fight me. Give in to your feelings. Your body wants mine."

"No." She shook her head, trying to break the curling effect on her mind and body. She wasn't going to let him influence her. "I belong to Alonso."

"He is nothing compared to me. I can give you an eternity of pleasure, making you the queen of my existence. I'd screw you like no other ever could. Night after night of worshipping your body over and over. Picture it, sweet Jolie."

His words matched the images of them in ecstasy, rolling in satin sheets as he fed off her body, caressing her every curve with his skilled hands, tasting each inch with his tongue.

It was almost too much, his hold over her mind—so strong it was draining. She didn't want to give in. As she wavered and her eyes fluttered closed, he leaned in and hungrily kissed her.

The kiss was nothing like what she had experienced with Alonso. This vampire, tempting with his tall, powerful essence, didn't raise her desires to the level she wished. She wanted her dark lover, her Alonso.

Within the recesses of her brain, she heard him cry in the distance, a menacing call of outrage.

Lucius broke the kiss, and Jolie knew he had also heard Alonso's angry scream.

With a swift wave of his hand, the crowd parted way like the Red Sea for Moses, forced aside by his powerful magic.

Picking her up, he cradled her in his arms and carried her through the club. At the door, the bouncer tried to stop him from taking her. An invisible force flung the mountainous man like a feather.

In the busy street, he carried her, determined to take her, her meager struggles nothing to him.

"Please, let me go. Don't do this," she pleaded.

"You're mine. I've waited too long for a worthy mate."

With supernatural strength, he sped through the streets. The speed dizzying, Jolie squeezed her eyes shut. They must have moved so fast no human could see them pass.

When he stopped, she opened her eyes and glanced around. It could be any number of cemeteries throughout the city. All aboveground tombs looked so similar, with the exception of Marie Laveau's, littered with the graffiti of believers.

"Here, I will make you a creature of the night and bind you to me for all eternity."

"He'll come for me."

"Not before I'm through. You'll be *my* life-mate, no other's."

"Why are you forcing this?" She placed a palm against his face, trying to calm the rage bubbling within his heart. He was lonely, hurting. She wanted him to understand. Fighting him would be of no avail, his strength in body and spirit overwhelming hers. She had to appeal to his aching heart.

He closed his eyes, inhaling her scent.

She asked gently, "Why, Lucius?" She knew why. She wanted him to admit to his weakness.

"Because I'm lonely. I need a woman to love." His voice lost power and revealed the vulnerability within.

"But I saw a woman in your future. She's coming. What if you make me your mate, then you meet her? Will you toss me aside, ruined in heart and soul? Can you live with the fact that

I'll forever see another's face in place of yours? My heart will always belong to another, no matter how much you wish it differently."

He released her from his hold, letting her stand on solid ground. The darkness encircled them within the City of the Dead. Only the sounds of insects cut the silence. She could understand why he wanted companionship as they stood in this isolated place.

Turning away from her, he lost some of the menacing aura surrounding him. "I've been alone for centuries. More than six hundred years ago, I met Alonso wallowing in his sorrow over a dead woman. I felt a connection to him and turned him that night. We traveled Europe for a century, feeding off the living, until he had enough of me. He had a different view of this existence, and that caused ripples in our relationship. We parted, but I deeply felt the loss of his friendship. I vowed to never let anyone hurt me again. But now," he sighed and looked back at her, "I need a life-mate."

"You won't take mine," Alonso said, stepping from the darkness. Wrapping his arms around Jolie, he kissed her forehead and whispered, "You okay?"

She nodded. "Just a bit shaken up."

"Lucius, you ever try something like this again, I swear, I'll drive a stake through your heart and leave you to burn away in the morning light."

Lucius began to walk away, but his sad voice echoed through the increasing shadows. "My friend, I may one day ask you to do just that."

There, in the midst of the cemetery, Jolie clung to Alonso, the danger gone. "He's very lonely, and his heart yearns for love."

"As all vampires eventually do. Finding our life-mate is the one purpose of our existence. If we don't find them after so many centuries, we lose hope."

"Like him."

He tipped her chin so she could gaze into his face. "And I found my life-mate. Jolie, will you sacrifice your mortality to be with me?"

"Become a vampire to love you for all eternity?"

He nodded.

"Hmm, hard question to answer." She broke away and began to pace, humor touching her voice. "Let me see. Nights filled with passionate sex with a sexy vampire for all time. Oh, sounds like torture to me." She turned to him. "Bring it on."

He laughed and scooped her into his arms. "Woman, I'm going to start those passionate nights tonight."

"Oh, so what was last night?"

"A trial."

Chapter Four

Back at her apartment, Jolie came to the conclusion she'd never get used to vampire speed. It left her lightheaded, but then, Alonso nibbling on her neck did that too.

"So how do you make me a vampire? Will I have to drink blood and all?"

Settling in bed after they stripped away their clothes, he took her into his arms. "I drink from you to the point of completion then you drink from me. It can be a sensual bonding between a male and female."

"How was it with Lucius?"

His hand stilled on her hip. "I was given little choice at the time. It was not a bonding of hearts like ours will be. I have a blood bond with Lucius, but not a life bond."

"And the drinking of blood?"

He groaned and rolled her atop him. She straddled his hips, his cock poised at her wet entrance. "I don't think I like the idea of you drinking from any man but me."

Leaning over, her erect nipples brushed his chest hair, coursing tiny thrills through her veins. "Mmm, I get to have you on my lips each night to survive?" She moved down his body, nipping along the way. She teased one nipple to tautness, then the other. He was delicious, and she wanted to taste all of him.

"Ah, sweet Jolie. I'd love to fill you each night."

She giggled as she nuzzled the valley between his nipples, the hair teasing her nostrils, filling her senses with his clean outdoor scent. "Are we talking sustenance here or something else?" she asked, playfully running her fingernails down his sides.

His entire body jumped under her fingertips. His breathing turned ragged and shallow. "Anything you want, I'll give it to you."

Slowly she moved lower, and his breathing became louder. He brought his hands to her head and gently held her between his palms.

"I want to drink from you in every way," he whispered. "I need to taste you."

She grasped his stiff length and caressed it. A small bead of moisture sat on the tip of the large purple head. Leaning over, she caught the drop with her tongue, and Alonso moaned in ecstasy. She glanced toward his face, his eyes closed and his mouth open, completely under her control.

The feeling of power over her lover intoxicated Jolie. She loved to see him give himself over to her. Bending down to the satiny-covered rod of hot steel, she closed her mouth over his cock and began to suckle. The salty taste of him made her drunk with want.

He held onto her head, guiding her to continue her loving. She teased his balls, testing their weight with one hand. He inhaled sharply at her movements, and she knew he was getting close. She took him deeper into her mouth and sucked harder. He screamed her name as he climaxed. She drank every drop, relishing the salty taste. He grasped her hair between his fingers as each wave of liquid sex shot from him.

Once his body had drained, he released her head, his arms flopping down upon the bed. She licked away every trace of his desire then positioned herself next to him. She draped her arm over his chest, playing with the dark hair that feathered him there.

The sound of his calm breathing was all she could hear. He held her teasing hand, keeping it steady. "Thank you. I've never experienced such euphoria as that."

"It's only the beginning, remember?" She led her hand down his abdomen and to his cock, already recovering and coming to attention once again. "Seems he may be ready for more."

In a flash of movement, he rolled her onto her back and pinned her arms above her head. "You're so fucking perfect for me." Then a tenderness passed over his features. "I love you, Jolie."

"I love you too." She moved her hips beneath him. "Make love to me and make me eternally yours."

"There may be some pain. But I'll be here to see you through."

"Okay."

She spread her legs wider, and he entered her in a slow thrust. She gasped and tugged at her arms, wanting to hold him closer, but he steadily held them above her head. He moved in easy, relaxed strokes, building the fire in an unhurried tempo. This wasn't just sex. It wasn't anything dirty or obscene. He made love to her and worshipped each leisurely penetration of her slick canal.

He stoked the flames, and Jolie thought she would die of the wondrous sensations building within her soul. She loved this man, this vampire, with all her heart. Her soul recognized him as the mate for which she had yearned. As the inferno began to flicker out of control and her body climaxed, he bit into her flesh above her left breast, sending her over the edge. She screamed his name and saw her world spin out of control with her orgasm. Alonso drank from her, and she welcomed it. He pumped his seed into her body as he took her life fluid.

Suddenly darkness and fear began to engulf her. Colors turned to black, and she felt her life drift away. Pain coursed through her body, and she thought she could not fight the encroaching dark.

Then a salty, metallic liquid touched her lips. Tasting the fluid, she welcomed it, drinking it into her mouth. Gulp after gulp, the warm substance renewed her strength.

When the source pulled away, she heard Alonso in the distance. "That's enough for now, little one."

She licked her lips and opened her eyes. Gazing down at her with dark eyes was the man she loved. She raised an unsure hand to his face and traced the slight stubble along his chin. "I love you," she whispered.

He leaned over and brushed his lips over hers. "I promise to love you forever."

* * * * *

Dazed, Jolie awoke within Alonso's arms. Nuzzling closer, she inhaled him. His clean scent seemed more intense, as though she could smell the crisp breeze of morning upon his skin.

Opening her eyes, she was amazed by the sheer clarity in the darkness. She could see every detail of the lacey curtains at the window, and the grain of the wood on a rocking chair across the room as well as the threads woven into the seat cushion upon it.

The smells around her—Alonso's skin and the musk of their lovemaking, mixed with the pine cleaner she'd used to mop the kitchen floor and the carpet deodorizer she sprinkled down a few days ago when cleaning—assaulted her nostrils. So many different smells.

Then she began to hear the littlest noises—from the wind blowing through a crack in the window to the scuffle of the tiny legs of a spider on the ceiling. She heard, saw and smelled everything so much more intensely.

"It is your vampire blood. This is the world experienced as a vampire. All the world about us is more tuned, clearer. You will learn how to adjust to the sensory overload of it all."

Alonso turned over in bed and stroked her cheek with his fingertips. "All of it isn't bad, you know."

"What do you mean? I don't know if I can take all this…clarity. It is a lot to take at once."

He leaned into her and her body hummed with awareness. "Sex is more stimulating as a vampire," he said in a husky voice. "The touch is heightened too."

She moaned. Sex was incredible with Alonso. How could sex as a vampire be more stimulating?

"Got a silk scarf?" he asked.

"In the dresser in the top left drawer."

He got out of bed and she admired his powerful grace as he moved across the room. The moonlight from the window danced over his silhouette. He found a scarf and headed back to bed.

"And what do you expect to do with that?" she asked with a giggle.

"A lesson in trust and seduction. Now come, kneel on the bed."

She did as he told her, her excitement increasing with each breath. She stilled as he covered her eyes with the silk, the soft cool fabric whispering against her skin. Even that smallest touch seemed amplified. She gasped softly.

His hard frame pressed against her backside and vulnerability washed through her body as he breathed against her hair next to her ear, "Reach out with your new senses. Smell me, taste me…*feel* me."

His hands moved slowly across her skin, fingertips tracing along in gentle glides, driving her senses wild. The fact that she couldn't see seemed to heighten her own sensitivity to his touch. Or was it her new vampiric senses? She didn't have the clarity of mind to analyze it with him touching her, his heat seeping into her body.

He remained close, his breath warm and alluring through her hair as he whispered again, "Just relax and enjoy my touching you. I'm going to love you with my fingertips and bring you to the heights of pleasure."

A shutter pumped through her veins as her heart skipped a beat. Lost in his touch and his promises, she moaned and leaned back into him. His one hand stayed upon her waist while the other glided across her skin. He palmed one of her breasts and she felt a rush of excitement pool between her legs. Testing the weight of her breast in his palm, he said in a husky voice, "You have beautiful breasts, my love." His thumb eased over her rosy peak and her womb clenched. "Mmm...yes. Perfect," he moaned.

His thumb stroked over her hard nipple as his fingers squeezed her breast gently. Meanwhile, his other hand splayed across her belly and slowly moved downward. He held her firmly to his body and she felt his cock, enlarged and straining, nestled between her buttocks. Its heat seared into her skin, like hot steel fresh from a forge. His fingertips dipped lower and brushed against the trimmed area of her mons. He groaned, a deep throaty sound, and he breathed warmly into her ear, "I love that you leave some of your precious pelt." He chuckled and the sounds sent shocks of awareness across her skin. Coupled with his fingers lightly massaging her pubis, it was driving her closer to the edge.

On her knees with her legs spread wide, she nestled further into his body. His muscled thighs framed hers, and she felt completely lost in his embrace.

Then his fingers slid through the wet folds, and she jumped beneath his touch. Open and naked, she was more than vulnerable, weakened to the point of surrender. She gave her body over to him, this man that glided into her life through magical means. He dominated her heart and her body, and she gave it all freely. Losing herself to this man was beyond any sexual relationship she'd ever experienced in the past. No man but Alonso could've ever awakened such longings in such a short time.

"So wet. Do I make you weep between your legs with want of me?" His voice was barely controlled. He had to be just as on edge as she.

"Yes," she croaked, her voice foreign to her ears.

His thumb grazed over her aching nubbin and she gasped. Her hands covered his, urging him to continue touching her. "I bet your sheath is so hot and tight right now, I could lose myself within your body." He pushed a finger up through her folds into her entrance and she shattered. Her body convulsed, drawing in his fingers further. He pumped in and out, prolonging her climax as he stroked her clit with his thumb.

As the orgasm receded into a calm satisfaction, Jolie slumped back, leaning her weight into his body. He pulled his fingers from her wetness and held her tightly, wrapping his arms about her body.

"I want to fuck you all the time, show you pleasure every night of our lives."

"Alonso, please, fuck me now."

He directed her to lie on her stomach and eased her hips into the air, her ass perfectly level with his cock. He rubbed the tip in her slick juices, and she cried aloud.

Alonso teased her pussy, and he entered her feminine passage into heaven. Leaning over her back, he reached around her with one hand to search with his fingertips for her clit. She groaned and pushed back against him, taking his penis into her deeper as he stroked her fleshy button with tender brushes.

As he thrust into her, her walls clamped down upon his length, milking him, sucking his cock further into her body. It took him beyond his dreams and into a land of salvation. Buried deep within her sheath, he found his peace.

Covering her with his body, he rejoiced in the intimate skin-on-skin connection. They moved as one, mating in wild passion and engulfing love and devotion.

As their tension built, each begging for release, she yelled and climaxed. His seed spilled into her as he joined her in climax.

But it wasn't enough.

The taste of her was too entrancing. He pumped into her cunt as he took hold of her shoulder with his mouth. Biting down, he held her in place, tasting her tangy blood upon his tongue. Rich, warm life-fluid exploded with flavor as he drank from her. One climax led into another as she gave her blood to her lover.

"You are my cherished one, Jolie. I have waited so long to find you," he whispered as he finished, licking the wound sealed and holding her within his arms.

A fatigue ached at her limbs, heaviness keeping her in place. It was as though an elephant sat on every joint.

"We'll have to seek our resting place soon," he whispered against her temple. "You're a fledgling now. Dawn will be very tiring for you."

"Where will we go? Do I have to sleep in a coffin?"

"Well, no. I do usually, but I will find us a new place to rest if you wish." He kissed her cheek and she sighed.

"Alonso, I will tell you—the thought of sleeping in a coffin creeps me out. Can't we do some sort of windowless room with a nice big bed?"

"Your wish, *mia amore*, is my command."

Chapter Five
Lucius

Sitting on the roof of the tomb of the Voodoo Queen, Lucius knew the moment Alonso turned Jolie into a vampire. He still wished she was his. But she had been right. What if the one destined to be his mate truly was still out there somewhere? Hundreds of years of waiting, and how much longer did he have to wait?

With a fingernail, he carved three Xs into the stone roof and knocked, the rumored way to make a wish to Marie Laveau. "Grant me my wish, bring me love everlasting."

A howl rang through the air. Lucius glanced up then closed his eyes, inhaling the scent of a beast in the distance. With his ultra-sensitive senses, he picked up the trail of a female wolf hunting in the far-off bayou. A wolf in the swamps of Louisiana? Alligators he could understand, but a wolf?

She howled into the night once again, a call of loneliness cutting through the dark. His heart ached for the beast, knowing all too well the pain she felt.

There was something odd about her scent. Something strange. He zeroed in on her location and watched her with his mind's eye. She sat upon a log underneath a great cypress. Magic and mystery surrounded her body, and she howled at the full moon yet again.

Could it be that this was no ordinary wolf?

As if sensing someone watching her, the beast turned and loped off into the black cover of twisted trees.

Lucius stood upon the roof of the tomb and gazed out over New Orleans toward the distant bayou, realization dawning.

Jolie had been right. His mate was out there…

And she was a werewolf.

* * * * *

The night air filled her lungs as she leapt over another fallen, rotting log. Moisture clung to her fur from the mist rising from the murky bayou. The strong scents of mud, wet wood and decaying foliage permeated her nostrils.

None of these familiar smells or sights could ease her troubled mind.

Someone was watching her.

Tala couldn't shake the feeling of an unknown observer piercing the darkness with his intense gaze. Her entire being shuddered at the experience, yet it wasn't entirely unpleasant. She could almost see him in her mind's eye, a tall, strong figure perched atop a stone building, gazing over the horizon. His long blond hair fluttered lightly in the breeze, but those crystal-blue eyes full of pain and wonder intrigued her.

The image had sprung to mind as she eyed her muddy domain. Within the deep Louisiana bayou she was queen, but the man made her feel vulnerable. It was a strange sensation, since she had lived her entire life in complete control.

She chose to live outside of human existence because of her double life. Born to shifter parents, she had been raised in isolation with her twin sister. It was better not to mingle too much with the humans anyway. They didn't understand the life of a shifter, nor were they capable of learning.

Most of her kind traveled in packs. She disliked the pack life. Pack politics always ensured the females remain subservient, and she couldn't live like that. Running with other werewolves was one thing, but allowing herself to be used only as a sexual vessel for breeding purposes wasn't for her.

Unlike in popular movies, a werewolf didn't retain its human form in any way. When Tala transformed into the beast, she was able to maintain her human awareness, but her body changed into that of an animal—the *loup garou*.

Werewolves could shapeshift at will anytime they wished. She could change into the wolf with the slightest thought or feeling. Sometimes the beast would fight to the surface, and her animalistic instincts took over. This was especially true during mating season. The urge to join with a male was so overpowering at times, she'd lose control during the actual act. Nothing like sinking her teeth into a man's shoulder as her body sang with a climax.

In human form, she retained some of the beast's instincts and animalistic reactions. If she interacted with a person she disliked, her entire being would rebel against the contact. Or if she felt attracted to a man, the beast would claw its way to the surface and demand sexual gratification, if only for temporary relief.

Wolves mated for life, and Tala had yet to meet her mate. She did relieve her sexual urges with those humans she found appealing, but none filled that empty place in her heart. Years of painful longing had gotten to her, part of the reason she lived in the bayou.

Leaping over another fallen log, she fought the rise of sexual fire within at the thought of the Viking god from her vision.

Then she sensed a new scent. A stranger within her domain. She sprinted in the direction of the intruder. Danger filled the air as she closed in on the new arrival.

Within the dark vines and wildly twisted roots of cypresses and other swamp vegetation, she spotted the white glow of fur. The beast stood still, his icy eyes staring at her. No, they pierced her—stripping away the external creature and baring the soul of her very being.

A white wolf. Not just any wolf, but one surrounded with ethereal magic and supernatural power.

Sniffing, she knew he wasn't one of the shifters, a *loup garou*. She would have immediately recognized the signature scent. He was different.

And still he stood, his pale coat reflecting the moonlight, making him appear heavenly. But an underlying sense of danger betrayed that image.

She stepped closer. With a low howl, she invited him to run with her. He answered with a bark. Even in this form, her body tingled with awareness.

He loped to her and licked her muzzle, then rubbed his strong body along hers in a sign of animalistic tenderness. His touch sent shivers of electric desire through her veins.

Mine, Tala heard, whispered in the recesses of her mind.

She returned his affectionate caresses by rubbing along his body. Strong and toned, he was a fine wolf. Playfully nipping at his neck, she started a game of tag and trotted off for him to chase her.

He did. They ran through the muddy land surrounding the swampy depths. With the humid air, dampness had settled over everything. Wet soil and leaves beneath her paws, and the male wolf by her side, made her feel alive and free. She remembered what it felt like to run with the pack, to belong. Now, to have a male so obviously wanting her was exhilarating. Running through the bayou with her was a sure way for him to come into her heart.

Something about him made Tala's heart race in tempo with the beating of their feet as they played tag. He'd chase her, then they'd reverse and she'd chase him. When they switched again, he tackled her in the wet foliage. Her body fell and she laughed, sounding like a hyena rather than a wolf.

He pinned her beneath him and rolled her onto her left side. They licked each other's faces, and Tala cherished their unexplainable connection.

Then he stilled and stared at her.

His weight increased, and his body shifted in size and shape.

No, he wasn't a shifter.

Worse—a vampire!

Now in human form, a handsome face stared down at her. A smile curved sensual lips, and blond hair fell about his head in long waves. Those same piercing eyes from her vision studied her—vampire eyes.

"Turn into human form, woman," he commanded, his voice strangely arousing.

Tala struggled beneath his hold, but his arms only tightened about her body and his legs firmly straddled her. Just then, she was painfully aware of his nudity. Naked and powerful.

"I said shift," he repeated.

Concentrating, she focused her lycan powers and began to shift. Fur turned to skin, paws changed to hands and feet, and an elongated wolfen face transformed into the features of a woman. Oddly enough, she never thought herself very appealing as a human but hoped he thought differently.

When the transformation ended, her naked body lay beneath his, intimately connected. Skin glided across skin. He groaned and shifted his position, nudging her legs open. His cock lay perfectly against her slick folds. With a slight movement of his hips, he could enter her.

Oh, God, yes…

"You're beautiful," he said simply. "What's your name?"

"Tala," she whispered, her voice raspy.

"I'm Lucius." He moved his legs, nudging her thighs open slightly more. "I want you, Tala."

She answered by wrapping her arms around his neck and pulling his head down. Against his lips, she said in a low voice, "Mate with me."

Colors swirled about her as he penetrated her slick core. He devoured her in a hungry kiss while his body commanded hers in a domination of her senses. He pounded into her body with a violent need to reach the pinnacle of pleasure, no tenderness, no gentility. Just raw, carnal savagery, bonding their bodies together in a fierce coupling.

She gasped with each invasion, squeezing his cock within her. His body slid over hers as a layer of sweat and the moist bayou air coated their skin. Crickets and other insects called into the night, the only other noises heard among their grunts, heavy breathing and the sound of flesh on flesh.

He broke his hungry kiss to roughly nibble her ear. Damn, he was everything she could ask for in a male.

No, your mate.

He whispered into her thoughts while holding her arms above her head with one hand. Her breasts pushed upward toward his body, and her nipples strained against his hard, muscled chest. His other hand cupped and fondled one of her breasts, squeezing her sensitive nipple between his fingers. She moaned and arched her hips upward, meeting his continued thrusts.

God, what a sensation. His entire body overwhelmed her, a sensual domination of her entire physical being. His powerful legs rubbed against her own, creating an awareness of his massive sexual prowess. How many women had sampled a fierce taking at this vampire's hands?

She tried not to surrender to her body's call to join with him, to shatter in his arms in an all-consuming orgasm. But the beast within her clawed—the animal begged for release. She needed to quake and come for this savage vampire who appeared in her domain to fuck her like no other male ever had or, she suspected, ever would.

His pace quickened. The thrusting grew more insistent. He released her arms and cradled her hips to receive his cock deeper. Yes, she needed to have him to the hilt, touching her inner walls, filling her hollow core. She clawed his shoulders with her fingernails, scraping his skin and drawing small amounts of blood.

God, yes, he matched her ferocious need to mate, to fuck. She wanted no words of love this night. She needed only a hard cock and a man who used it with expert skill.

As her cunt clenched tightly around his length, she howled into the night with each spasm of her muscles in orgasm. She needed to milk him, wanting more as each erotic sensation washed over her.

He united with her in the frenzied joining, spilling his hot seed into her in spurts. He yelled in primal delight then savagely bit into her shoulder, deep and hard.

At his bite, she screamed as another orgasm shook her. He drank her blood, a soothing sensation. She wanted to be bonded to this incredible vampire, this blond demon who ravaged her body upon the moist earth and foliage.

The crashes of pleasurable desire ebbed, and he released his teeth from her skin. He licked the sore spot, more tenderly than expected after such an animalistic coupling.

"So sweet and rich," he said against her skin. "And all mine."

"A bit sure, are we?" She stroked away his soft, silky blond hair from her neck, so long it practically wrapped her in its own embrace.

He leaned upward, breaking the welcome feel of his body on hers. "Very sure, Tala. You're my mate. You shall be mine for all eternity."

"What do you mean, 'all eternity'?"

"I shall make you as I, a vampire."

"I can't," she said, a tear welling in her eye.

"Why not?" His voice told of his growing anger.

"Because the blood mix of a *loup garou* and a vampire is forbidden. I can die from the change."

"And how do you know this?"

"I saw it happen to my sister."

"What do you mean?" He rolled onto their earthen bed at her side.

"She fell for a vampire about five years ago, when we lived in the Okeefenokee swamp in Georgia. They exchanged the blood bonds, thinking they would be joined forever. But something went wrong. We didn't know what caused the reaction, but it proved fatal, even to her superior strength."

* * * * *

Lucius stroked Tala's rich auburn hair. He needed to shed light on the entire situation. How could the gods see him mated to one that was forbidden to him? "What exactly happened to your sister?"

"The reaction of the mix between vampire and werewolf blood drove her over the edge, killing her and condemning Damon, her lover, to eternal pain and loneliness." At Lucius' questioning expression, she explained further, "The chemical reaction in the brain causes a metaphysical imbalance. The brain can't handle the imbalance and mental instability occurs."

"But how did she die from this?"

"The body fights to correct this but in turn releases toxins into the bloodstream, causing death." She paused, then with tears in her eyes, she said, "There is no known treatment, no cure."

"I'm sorry, Tala." He meant the words, his heart wrenching at her pain. How many centuries had he not cared for another? The emotion almost seemed foreign. Yet at this moment, he did care for her, wishing she'd not feel the loss of her sister.

"I am centuries old and never paid much mind to the myths and legends of my kind. Vampire lore is so saturated with human fear, I never know what is true and what is merely fantasy," he said, tracing her jaw with his fingertip.

"I'd heard tales of my kind trying to mix with vampires but never thought them more than bedtime stories to frighten children. At least, I didn't believe until I saw it happen to my sister and Damon."

"We will beat this. You are my mate—nothing can keep me from claiming you." *My mate.* It ran through his mind, and he could hardly believe it. After all this time, he held his mate.

And so beautiful. Fiery hair framed her face and fell softly down her back and around her shoulders. A man could lose a day just absorbing those silken hairs between his fingers. And her skin, flawless and slightly tanned, gave her entire body an exotic hue. The most interesting features were her eyes—deep, emerald green, like a grassy hillside in Ireland. He could see her there among the stony walls, her eyes perfectly matching the luscious greens surrounding her.

Her body was made to entice him, with curves in all the right places. God, he hated the idea of any other man touching her, but from this moment on, none would get the chance.

Sliding his hand over the firm swell of her breasts, tipped with dark brown areolas and even darker nipples, he watched in curiosity as her skin reacted to his touch. Yes, he could spend another entire day just worshipping those taut beauties with his tongue and mouth.

Unfortunately, time grew short. He could feel the dawn's approach, having existed within its shadow for so long. "Tala, I must seek my rest, for morning swiftly approaches."

She groaned and curled into his embrace. By the gods, she was perfect. So responsive, so tender—and she met his fierce need with her own wild instincts, recognizing him as her mate.

But what of this curse of insanity? They needed to explore that more. Restraining his urge for her to drink from him, however, would be extremely difficult. He needed to have her. He had just found her after centuries and would do anything to keep her.

"I wish you wouldn't leave," she said in a low voice, nuzzling his neck.

"I must. But tomorrow night, I shall find you and we'll talk of this curse of which you speak. Maybe together we can search for an answer."

"I only wish you were right, Lucius."

"There are those who can help. Don't lose hope so quickly. We've been brought together and I intend to keep you. Let me check with some who may know more of this curse, then I'll come to you."

With that, he caught her face with his hand and kissed her. It was unlike their earlier kisses. This was gentle and emotional. Promise laced the very movement of his lips over hers, and he wished for more time this night to explore her body's wonders.

As he bent away from her and stood, his body screamed in protest. Even after plunging into her, he was ready to take her again. His rock-hard erection jutted out from his body, and he forced himself to turn and step away.

He shifted into the form of a large raven. Being an ancient, Lucius had the ability to shift at will into any form he wished. Change in size and shape took more concentration than ever before, since he wished to dive into Tala once again. After the crackling of his transformation died away, he flapped his wings and flew, perching briefly in a nearby tree to take one last look at his mate.

She had shifted into her wolf form and looked magnificent. What would it be like for them to mate as wolves? Someday he'd find out, but not now. He had to seek shelter.

Reluctantly, he spread his wings and lifted off into the night.

As he soared away from the swamp, he heard upon the wind the mournful cry of his mate, calling him back to her side.

Chapter Six

The next evening, when Lucius emerged from his tomb in the great St. Louis Cemetery, he sniffed the wind, looking for Tala.

Tala—the Native American word meaning wolf. Such an appropriate name for a beauty such as her. He had sampled only some of her the evening before, but planned on more of the same tonight.

That is, once he looked into this curse of mixing vampire blood with that of the *loup garou*.

Against his better judgment, he went to the one place where the vampires converged. They drank and partied in complete secrecy from the humans in New Orleans. He'd known of the Devil's Talon but had never appeared there, preferring a lonely existence instead of making vampire buddies.

Down an alley off Canal Street, he approached the spell-covered entrance to the exclusive club. The doorman slid open the peephole, gasped, then slammed it shut. For a minute, Lucius thought he'd been denied entry, but the door opened slowly and the protection spell dropped away.

"Wait," the doorman, a burly vampire, said. "I know you're up to no good. What do you want here?"

"I need to find some answers regarding the curse of mixing vampire and *loup garou* blood. I'd hoped someone here could help."

The man reluctantly allowed him entrance. Behind him, as the door slammed, Lucius felt the protection spell close off the human world from this far more dangerous vampiric haunt.

Even in the early evening, the club had a good crowd. Lucius could smell the warm and sweet Bloody Marys being served to the patrons. How any could prefer a meal served in a glass as opposed to fresh from the vein was beyond him.

The music coursed and pumped from the loud speakers, and vampires moved to the deafening beat. He wondered how their extra-sensitive hearing dealt with all the noise. Lucius had had more time and experience to learn to filter noise, but still, he only used clubs such as these as hunting grounds. He preferred the quiet stillness of the bayou.

Many near him stopped dancing and stared. Obviously, his reputation preceded him. Vampires had learned to fear him. That would all change now that he'd found his mate.

But what if the curse was true? Would drinking his blood bring Tala insanity and eventually death?

He doubted he could exist without her now that he'd mated with her. She would be the only string of balance in his existence. If he lost her he'd meet the dawn, and gladly so.

"What are you doing here?" Alonso asked as Lucius approached his table.

"I need advice." Lucius knew he looked menacing in his typical black suit and holding his silver-tipped walking stick. He was of the Old World, and modern T-shirts and jeans didn't suit him.

Jolie sat with Alonso, as did two other male vampires. "You found her, didn't you?" she asked, still lovely and tantalizing. Her beauty and inner psychic power had initially drawn him to her. Alonso was lucky to have her as a mate.

"Yes, but there is a problem."

"What?"

"She's a werewolf."

Alonso and the two males moaned.

"What does that mean?" Jolie asked as Lucius took a chair and sat next to her.

"It means they can't exchange the blood bonds to unite them for eternity," one of the males said, another Italian with short black hair and an accent that probably drew females like sugar. "Legend has it the mixing of blood between vampire and werewolf is forbidden. To do so will reap insanity, and eventually death, for the werewolf."

"Thus condemning the vampire to eternal pain and loneliness," finished the other male, a dark blond with a clipped British accent.

Lucius knew he had come to the right place, even though Alonso watched him with suspicion. Lucius couldn't blame him. After all, only last night he had stolen away Jolie and tried to force her to be his.

It all seemed like so long ago. Now Lucius had Tala. But…

"Is there anything that can be done to counteract the curse?" he asked.

"I've heard of no solution to prevent the insanity," the blond said. "I'm Raife, by the way."

The other Italian vampire added, "And I'm Leonardo."

Lucius nodded at them then turned to Jolie. "Do you know anything that could possibly help us?" He took her hand in his, her flesh warm to the touch. "Please, we need…I need to keep her. She's my mate. I've waited so long to find her. I can't lose her now."

Sadness touched her eyes as she squeezed his hand. A menacing growl from Alonso made Lucius release her. No sense getting into a battle with her mate.

"Let me look into a few things." She paused, then a light shown in her eyes. "Have you thought of visiting a voodoo priestess?"

"What good will that do?" Leonardo asked. "They hate us. To them, we're evil creatures."

"How about a vampire voodoo priestess?"

Just then, a cappuccino-skinned woman with large dark eyes approached the table. "What?" she asked as they all gazed at her.

"I believe our voodoo priestess has arrived," Alonso quipped. "Know anything about the vampire-werewolf curse?"

"Ah, yes. Question is, do you know how it came about?" Monique's question was met with silence, so she continued. "Centuries ago, Transylvania hosted the dark races of lycanthropes, werewolves and vampires—those who hunted at night within the Carpathian Mountains. One night, a female wolf, Sabina, encountered the vampire master, Victor. Instead of a struggle for power and supremacy, as was each of their species' instincts, they mated. Instantaneous attraction brought these two unlikely lovers together. They shared nights of passion and sex, loving without care for the rest of their clans.

"Eventually, Sabina became pregnant. The act was so heinous in the eyes of the vampire and wolf clans, they called upon the powers of darkness that created them and laid a curse upon the forbidden couple. The mixing of bloods would cause such pain and insanity, then death.

"Sabina died with her unborn child. Victor lamented her death and met the morning's sun with his bride by his side."

"Do you think magic could help break the curse? Centuries of longing for my mate—if I lose her now, I won't hesitate to greet the dawn like Victor," Lucius said with sincerity.

"Understand, as far as I know, this has never been done," Monique began. "The mating of vampires and werewolves has long been forbidden, but we can try to remove the curse in a ceremony. It won't be easy. We are dealing with dark powers brought forth by the devil."

"We were meant to break this curse. Our love is strong. I recognized her as my life-mate and would fight the devil to keep her." Lucius was determined. No curse from jealous ancients was going to keep him from claiming Tala.

"If you think your love is strong enough to fight the curse, then we have a powerful weapon already," Monique said, placing her hand upon his shoulder.

For the first time all evening, Lucius felt hope. "When can we do this?"

"Tomorrow night. Bring your mate to this address." She pulled a card from a small purse and handed it to him. "I'll have everything ready."

"Need us to come?" Leonardo asked.

"Not necessary. If something goes wrong, I'll call," Monique replied.

If something goes wrong? The worst thing Lucius could think of was losing his newly found mate.

* * * * *

Tala paced the wooden porch of her swamp shack. Located deep in the bayou, it kept her isolated, the way she preferred.

An alligator emerged within the swamp and skidded across the still water, leaving ripples in its wake. They were also solitary creatures, not traveling with others of their kind. She felt closer to the gator than another werewolf.

Loneliness filled her, surrounded her with its painful curse. She found her mate in a Viking vampire, and they were to be denied the consummation of their bond. How could she fall so quickly for one so dangerous? Just loving him could cost her life.

The sun had set hours ago, and she knew he had risen from his rest. She could almost feel his onslaught of emotions regarding the curse. He was seeking an answer, but she had doubts anything could remove the destined insanity their blood bond would cause.

"Do not lose hope, my Tala. I may have found someone to help."

His thoughts became a comforting caress through her mind.

"Come to me, my mate. I need to have you near. I need your strength," she whispered back to him in her thoughts.

"Coming. We'll talk of this."

"We'll talk after we've mated. My body aches for you."

"As does mine."

Her body hummed as his mental touch eased through her mind and across her skin. She gasped as he cupped her breast with an invisible palm through the thin fabric of her dress. *"How can you touch me and not be here?"* she asked, grasping the porch railing for leverage.

"I'm an ancient of my kind, and I wish to touch you. I will do so with my magic if I can't physically."

With that, he tweaked her nipple, making it taut beneath his caress. She moaned, and in the recesses of her mind, heard him laugh.

"Oh, you're so evil," she sent back with a mental chuckle.

"You don't know how bad I can be, sweet."

She could hear the smile in his voice. Then his magical caress dipped lower over her abdomen. He still teased her nipples to aching berries, but he also held her hips and eased down over the apex of her thighs. God, it was like he had eight hands, touching, examining, driving her to ecstasy.

She raised one of her legs onto the porch railing, allowing him access to her core. Her juices flowed, hot and slick, moistening the crotch of her panties and preparing her body for his intimate contact. Or his intimate magical touch.

"Ah, I can almost smell your perfume, so exotic...so fuckable..." His invisible fingers touched her throbbing clit.

"Lucius," she called aloud. Her clothes an unwanted barrier, Tala pulled the dress over her head and yanked down the offending fabric of her underwear to stand naked. Only alligators and frogs witnessed her surrender. A cool breeze caressed her flesh, but it did nothing to ease the burning within.

Still, Lucius stroked her nubbin, driving her closer to the edge with each pass. Tala felt the phantom fingers slide through her slick folds, sampling her, tantalizing her. Holding onto the wooden railing, she arched her back while his unseen hands worshipped her entire body.

Her heart raced, pumping blood through her veins, along with the increasing thrills of the experience. Consumed with desire for her vampire, she wished herself beneath him, his penis plunging into her body, bonding them in the physical sense.

"Ah, sweet, I'm on my way, soaring above the bayou, coming to you. You're so ready for me, and I wish to taste your sweet center like a human would a fruit tart. I'll lick away every bit of the sweet cream then eat the entire treat, relishing the texture and taste on my tongue. Then I'll enter you and pound into that tightness until we both scream in passion…"

She moaned in frustration. *"Where are you? Damn it, get here!"*

He chuckled and thrust his phantom fingers deep into her canal. She screamed as her muscles contracted in climax. She couldn't hold out, and her body reacted to his touch and seductive words in wave after wave of orgasm.

As Tala began to recover from the overwhelming spasms racking her body, arms wrapped her into a warm embrace. She became aware of the warm, naked body pressed against her backside, the erect penis nestled between her butt cheeks.

This was no illusion. This was her mate, her lover, there, holding her.

"You're my every dream, every hope, every wish, Tala," he breathed into her ear, his hot breath sending chills down her spine.

She leaned back into his warmth. "Lucius, is there hope for us?"

"Tomorrow, we are to meet in town to take part in a ceremony to rid us of the curse."

"A ceremony?"

"A voodoo priestess will perform a ritual. A *vampire* voodoo priestess."

"That should be interesting," she quipped, humor tainting her voice.

"Yes, I'm curious too. At this point, it's our only hope." His fingertips traced the outer curves of her breasts.

She sighed at the trickles of excitement shooting through her entire being. "How can we be so connected after one meeting?"

"Your body recognizes mine as its mate, just like mine knows yours. We have been bound together by chance and destined for each other since the moment of our creation."

She turned in his arms to face him. Cupping his strong jaw in her hand, she said, "But we hardly know one another. Tell me about you. How did you become a vampire?"

Lucius sighed as he pulled her close, cradling her head to his chest. "My name was Loki the Strong to my people, and I was captain of my ship and made a living like many Norsemen at the time—through foreign invasion. One night my crew was raiding a village in the land now called Ireland. I stayed behind on the ship with my brother. Then out of the darkness, *he* swooped in on us." He paused and she held him tighter.

"You don't have to tell me more if you don't want to."

Stroking her hair, he continued, "Rourke was an Irish demon of the night. I saw him feast upon Johann with a viciousness new to me. As a Norseman, I'd seen plenty of death and gore, but this…this was brutal. As Johann lay upon the deck gasping for breath, his body nearly drained, the vampire turned to me. I pleaded with him to spare my brother. There was only one way to save him."

"Oh, dear God."

"I asked him to make Johann a vampire. I remember Rourke's eyes, blood red and on fire with evil. He accepted, only if I was willing to sacrifice my own life to become a vampire also."

"Rourke wanted you to become a vampire? Why?"

"One day I asked him that very question, and he said he'd watched us as we approached the island. He'd intended to kill us all. When I begged for my brother's life, he'd felt sorrow. Actually *felt* pain at his actions."

At her silence, he continued. "I swore to do whatever Rourke wanted, all to save Johann." He took a shaky breath and said, "I loved my brother. He was everything to me. I just couldn't let him die. I offered myself to Rourke in payment for Johann's life, even if he was to become a demon of the night."

"Did your brother survive?"

Lucius nodded solemnly. "Yes, Rourke turned him. I saw his neck heal before my eyes, and then it was my turn. I let Rourke take my human life in exchange for saving Johann. When it was over, Johann and I left the ship behind to go with Rourke. I hated him for what he did, but he was our only hope to survive. Rourke taught us the ways of the vampire, to hunt by night and rest by day. As our strengths grew, my brother and I planned to return to our home. But what was left for us there? Nothing. As men, we'd be heroes, welcomed by our village to celebrate our virility and cunning. But as vampires…" Lucius' voice trailed off, his face twisted in pain as he remembered his past.

Tala laid a comforting hand upon his arm. "As vampires, you were both considered evil."

He nodded. "We couldn't return to our village. Johann had no woman waiting for him. He had only me in the world. And I—I didn't want to go back and face Una."

"Una?"

Sadness etched his face, and he inhaled slowly, as though his immortal body needed to ease the sorrow of his soul. "My betrothed. We were to be joined upon my return. I didn't want to hurt her any more. By the time I was ready to strike out on my own, away from Rourke, she would have learned I was missing, presumed dead. She was right, and I didn't have the heart to show her what I'd become."

"Where did you both go then?"

"We traveled the world, first going to England. It was a fine hunting ground, but we didn't stay long, traveling across the channel to France, Spain, Portugal, Germany and further into Western Europe. While in Romania, Johann decided to go back to our country. I didn't want to go back—the memory of Una was too painful for me to even set foot into Norway."

"You never went home?"

"No. I began to grow bored of the life, if you can call it that. I wanted more. I started joining in local wars, playing games with life and death. It was during this time that I met the man who showed me what a demon truly was."

"Who?" Tala listened to his tale, trying to envision the history and events he'd seen during his long time on earth. It was staggering to think of how much he'd experienced in comparison to her.

"The Prince of Wallachia, better known as Vlad Tepes III. He used to call himself Draculea, the son of the dragon. He had a taste for the gruesome, and as one of the commanders in his army, I witnessed many thieves and beggars sentenced to the stake. He took an interest in me and my strength. I never told him my secret as to why I sought the darkness of night as my time to attack. Two centuries later, I would meet up with Vlad in the squalor of Whitechapel. He was drawn there by the stories of the Ripper."

"I thought Dracula was just a character Bram Stoker made up, using Vlad as his inspiration."

"True, but I often wonder if Stoker wasn't inspired in a more direct fashion."

She sat in awe looking at him. According to his accounts, Lucius was a vampire before the Norman Conquest, right on through to the time Jack the Ripper stalked Whitechapel and beyond.

"I know—it is a lot to take in. But that is my tale, the shortened version."

"Is Johann still around?"

"He's in France, joined with his life-mate there. The woman is leader of a coven in Paris. Johann seems to be content."

"And what happened to Rourke?" She shivered in his arms.

"He and I met some years later. He had changed since that first night so long ago. He has his life-mate to keep the beast from rearing to the surface."

"Is that what life-mates do? Tame the beast?"

"Partly. Those destined for each other through love and acceptance are life-mates. There is no denying the strength of the bond of life-mates. Balance and stability makes existence less torturous." He gazed down at her face and smiled. "You balance me. You are my life-mate, the one I've longed for, the one I ached for. I will love you with every cell of my being. I will protect you and all I ask is for your love in return."

"Make love to me, Lucius."

His mouth covered hers in a gentle kiss. The tender mingling of lips almost caused Tala to burst with joy. For the first time in her life she was in love, and this vampire held her heart within his grasp. He was her mate, her man, her life. In such a short time, he had become her reason to go on, the purpose in her isolated life.

She ran her fingers through the silky strands of his hair. He moaned into her mouth as she pressed him closer. She couldn't get close enough. She wanted to have him consume her, take her, love her.

He broke the kiss and dipped down to pick her up. Cradling her in his arms, he carried her into the small shack, basically a large room with all the necessities of life—a small kitchen with a café-style table and two chairs, a bed and a couch. The simple, full-size bed was covered with standard, no-frills sheets and blankets. On the walls hung oil paintings of wolves and Native Americans in the Old West. Against one wall a small bookcase stood full of books.

"You like to read a lot?" he asked, easing her onto the white cotton bedspread.

"Yeah, romances." She added with a laugh, "Mainly about werewolves finding love."

He chuckled as he covered her body with his. His weight was welcome, warming and comforting. "Ever read about a vampire falling for a werewolf?"

"Seems to be a favorite theme."

He nibbled the curve of her neck where it met her collarbone. She never knew that area was so sensitive or erotic. Shots of flaming excitement coursed through her when his teeth grated across her skin.

"And how do all these romances turn out?"

"Always happily ever after," she replied.

"So will we. We'll find a way to be together, even if it is only for a lifetime."

"I'd rather it be an eternity."

His body moved along hers, his hard planes in contrast to her softer curves. They fit together like pieces to a puzzle. His cock grazed her thighs. She opened to him so he could fit into her completely. Her body ached for him to join with her. She needed to have him fill her.

But he hesitated. Moving further down, he kissed along her abdomen and over her mons. His hot breath teased her cunt, aching with each touch of his hands upon her body.

He placed a kiss above her clit, and she whimpered. Just a bit further down, she wished.

"Heavenly scent," he breathed, the heat spreading over her skin as his hands moved across her body. He cradled her hips then gently felt his way up her body. Lucius mapped her body with his fingertips, and she fell into sheer ecstasy at his skillful caress. He worshipped her body with his hands, strong yet yielding to her every curve, every plane.

At the first flick of his tongue over her clit, she screamed, bucking her hips upward. She had no real control over her reactions to his touch. His lips closed over her nubbin, sucking the swollen flesh into his mouth.

She laced her fingers through his hair, steadying his head over her cunt, the suction upon her clit driving her wild. His tongue tantalized the tip in quick, little tastes, sending her body further into ecstasy. She approached the point of painful pleasure, almost climaxing before he eased the pressure, slowing his licks, calming her only to build her up again.

Tala was more than aware of the magic his hands worked upon her body. His every movement, every touch calculated to pleasure her. He passed his tongue slowly over the sensitive surface of her clit then began to explore the folds of her labia.

His fingers grazed lightly over her nether lips and she cried out. He commanded her body, her responses. With each pass of his lips against her, she thought she'd die of sexual delight. She wanted more but loved the way he held her at bay—denying her completion.

"Lucius," she whimpered. She wanted to please him, return the loving he gave with his mouth upon her cunt. She wanted to taste him, take him into her mouth, to feast upon the man that changed her world.

She pushed upon his head and he raised his lips from her weeping center.

"Don't you like it, Tala?"

"Oh I do," she admitted breathlessly. "But I want to give you pleasure too."

"I love driving you to the point where you think you can't return then bringing you back down."

"Evil man."

He chuckled, and the sound only excited her more. "Lucius…please!" The idea of sucking on him as he licked her was too delicious to ignore.

"What do you have in mind?" he asked.

She directed him to lie next to her. "Just lie on your back."

He did as he was told, and she rose from the bed and lifted one leg over him, straddling his body to face his cock, her cunt directly above his face.

"Oh now, there is a beautiful sight. Pink pussy, wet and ready for me." He grasped her thighs and steadied her over him as he began to lick her slick entrance.

Leaning over him, she grasped his cock in her hands. Long and thick, with a purplish head, it was a work of art. A small droplet seeped from the tip and she licked the salty substance away. He groaned and increased his pace upon her clit. His tongue danced over her flesh, and she matched his movements upon his cock. Tracing the length of him, she vowed then to memorize every inch of this man—this vampire.

When he plunged his tongue deep into her, she took him deeply into her mouth. He teased her clit with one thumb while testing the tight muscles of her anus with his other. She sucked harder upon his penis, relishing the pleasure she gave to him as he gave pleasure to her.

Love. She loved him. All her heart and soul wrapped about him in love—an all-consuming love coupled with a fiery passion unlike any she'd ever experienced. How could their love be forbidden? Surely their love and devotion could break any curse.

She didn't need to hear him say the words to know his feelings. No man would do the wonderful deeds he was doing now without some depth of emotion. She doubted the feel of his fingers caressing her rear entrance could be anything but exquisite. Everything he did to her was born of love.

The *demoni* had been tamed—by a wolfen mate.

He pressed a finger slowly through the puckered opening of her anus and she screamed as her orgasm ripped through her body. Everything seemed to snap at once. Muscles danced in the sexual rhythm of climax under the control of her sensual maestro. She felt every convulsion—each ripple of ecstasy—shimmy and shudder through her, from the tips of her toes to the top of her head. And all she could do was scream around his cock in her mouth.

Just when she thought rapture had its limits, he flipped her over onto her back. In a flash, he positioned himself between her legs. When Lucius slid into her slick wetness, Tala gasped, thinking her heart would burst. Emotions overflowed as he completed her entire being. This was what had been missing from her life. She had been lonely, but she had never realized how important a mate would be.

Slowly, he entered and retreated, rocking his hips with hers in a relaxed beat. Tears welled in her eyes at the sheer beauty of their joining. It wasn't a physical need, not lust—it was deeper, much more soul-touching than sex.

Running her hands over his toned back, she whispered her heart's desire, her inner feelings, never heard by any other creature. "I love you, Lucius. Please—love me too."

He stopped moving.

She had an instant of worry until she looked at his face.

He breathed the words Tala never thought any other would say to her. "I love you too, my sweet Tala."

They sealed their proclamations with a hungry kiss, and the tempo of their mating increased. The need to reach that pinnacle of heavenly bliss that lay within their grasp.

Then her body quaked, sending her soaring into paradise with him close behind. He grunted with each thrust, his pace quickening before finally finding release, joining her in a love-induced orgasm.

Colors burst behind her eyelids, visions of running in a beautiful meadow with Lucius at her side. As wolves, they were perfectly matched. He was her mate for life, there was no other. Curse or no, they were destined to remain together. Love would see them through. Love would be their weapon to defeat the powers keeping them from their destiny.

As Lucius calmed, he eased downward, relaxing upon her body. His breathing slowly returned to normal, as did the pace of his pumping heart. Raining light kisses across her hairline, he whispered his love and devotion.

Tala would never feel heartache again. She glowed within his embrace, wishing away the beams of morning so she may enjoy the newfound love of her vampire lover.

* * * * *

Just before dawn, Lucius had to seek his rest. He hated leaving Tala, especially when she lay naked, tempting him even while asleep against the soft bedcovers.

Before leaving, he covered her body with the sheet and tenderly kissed her temple.

"Tonight, my love, we shall break this curse that keeps us from the ultimate bond as mates."

Turning, he stepped onto the wooden porch overlooking the swamp waters. An alligator sat silently within the nearby reeds. He sent a mental command for it to protect Tala. Assured of its compliance, Lucius shifted into a raven. The air snapped with electric charges as his body transformed in size and shape.

He flew toward his resting place. Tomorrow night, Tala would rest with him. Never again would he have to sink into the deep sleep without the woman of his heart within his arms.

Lucius glided over the cemetery and spotted Alonso and Jolie slipping into their tomb to escape the coming sun.

Yes, his wait would soon be over.

Chapter Seven

Once the sun went down, Lucius arose refreshed and ready.

And hungry.

It was then he realized he hadn't fed off Tala last night.

Was there a meaning behind it? He wasn't sure.

While seeking his meal in a few humans, he discovered he had no desire to take their lives when he drank their blood. What was happening to him? Could love change him so completely?

As the last human staggered off and Lucius licked his lips of blood, he realized how much he preferred Tala's sweet blood. It tasted different than a human's, and he wanted to sample her again.

As he was about to contact her to meet him at the edge of the bayou so they could travel to the ritual, Lucius sensed a stranger was with her.

Another vampire was with Tala.

In a fury, Lucius shifted. As the great raven with inhuman speed, he soared across the early evening sky. On the wind, he caught the vampire's scent, one he didn't recognize.

As he approached the shack, he saw Tala with a tall, dark vampire. She looked irritated, and they appeared to be arguing.

"Tala, you know what can happen. Think of what happened to Telia," the vampire said as he paced the porch.

Lucius landed behind Tala and shifted into human form. Sometimes, like now, it was handy to be able to conjure clothes. He stood dressed in his immaculate black suit and held his walking stick. She backed into his waiting arms for comfort.

"Damon, I presume?" Lucius whispered to her, and she nodded confirmation.

"And you must be Lucius." Damon was a tall, blond-haired vampire with a muscular build. He had a telltale American accent with a slight Southern drawl. Obviously not an ancient vampire.

"Yes, and why are you here?"

"I felt trouble and I came right away."

"How could you feel trouble with my mate?"

"Because I loved and bonded to her twin."

Lucius enclosed Tala flush against his body, crossing her front with his walking stick, protecting her and soothing her shivering body. "We're going to try and overcome the curse with the help of magic."

"What magic is powerful enough to rid an ancient curse such as the one that condemned my Telia to death?"

"The magic of true love," Tala answered confidently.

Damon stood in silence then turned away. His shoulders slumped in defeat, or perhaps with painful memories. "I loved Telia. More than any other."

"And I love Tala. We're willing to take this risk." Lucius planted a soft kiss against her temple.

"Come with us," Tala offered.

"No, you go and try to break the curse. I only wanted to give you a warning. But maybe if your love is strong enough, there is hope."

"And if it doesn't work," Tala turned in Lucius' arms, "I ask for you to end my life before the madness completely takes hold."

Lucius felt humbled. "Tala, you must believe in this ritual. That is of great importance. Otherwise, it's doomed from the beginning. No doubts. We will beat this together."

"Tala, listen to him," Damon said. "Go with him. I wish you luck. But before I go, listen to me. Once you are bitten, it will take a few hours for your body to react to the blood mix. The process may be slow at first, but once the toxins are released, the effect can accelerate. You will slip into unconsciousness and have terrible visions—delusional, frenzied, driving you over the edge as the phantom pack calls to you, beckoning for you to join them."

"How do you know all this?" she asked.

"I held Telia as she slipped away. She called out to the pack while I held her unconscious body. They took her away from me, and I was helpless to fight them."

Damon stepped toward Tala. She left Lucius' arms and hugged her sister's lonely mate.

In a flash of black fur, Damon fled to prowl the bayou in search of something to ease his pain. As she watched him disappear into the dense trees, Tala felt his depression.

"Come, sweet," Lucius said. "They await us to start the ceremony."

Before leaving, the echo of Damon howling a sad, lonely song touched her soul. Tala prayed she would survive and not let Lucius exist in similar desolation. She knew they shared a bond already, and if broken, only extreme pain would follow.

* * * * *

At the small voodoo shop, Monique allowed them in the back door. She led them into a side room, where candles of various scents mixed in the air. Lucius tried to block out the perfumes wafting through his senses. How can a vampire endure such an assault on the nose?

Monique, dressed in long, flowing white robes and a turban, looked the part of a voodoo priestess. Lucius still felt leery. Much lay in the hands of this woman—his future, and Tala's.

The priestess took them into a circle of candles and instructed them to lie side by side.

"You must trust in one another. Let your love shine through any doubts or negative forces. The evil feeds off those negatives. The only way to fight for your greatest desires is to banish all evil from your hearts. Show your love."

"Are you saying we should make love? Here?"

"If it deems necessary, yes. I ask that you act on your innermost feelings. I will do the rest and call upon the spirits to help banish the evil that curses your joining."

With that, she stepped toward a tall basket and removed the lid. She pulled out a large white snake. Its hiss vibrated through the room.

"I'm scared, Lucius."

He gazed at Tala and saw fear in her eyes.

"Fear is one of those negative energies," Monique said. "Perish those fears, and concentrate on the positive. Think of being in his arms." She went to the door and called in several humans of African decent, who formed an outer circle.

Humans. It struck Lucius as odd. He thought they hated his kind.

But then he focused on Tala. "I'm here. We're doing this together." He took her hand and placed a kiss in her palm. "Think of how we meld when the passion overtakes us."

The drums and music began as the helpers struck up the beat. Monique began to dance, invoking the spirits.

Music pulsed through the room. Monique continued to dance and sing, holding the snake about her neck.

Lucius moved closer to Tala and half lay upon her. As he looked into her eyes, his emotions overwhelmed him. She had become everything to him in such a short while. How could there be anything negative in their union?

"I love you, Tala," he breathed, then closed his lips over hers.

Colors swirled around him as she readily responded. She opened her mouth to him, brushing her tongue along his in a sensual dance, matching the tropical beat surrounding them.

Words hardly seemed adequate to express his depth of feeling for her. A simple statement could be said by anyone, but he felt it in his heart. Pain, hunger, longing, delight, happiness. Yes, even happiness had crept into the dark heart of the *demoni scuri*. Legendary Lucius, former leader of a Viking horde, was humbled and at the mercy of a woman and her gentle heart and her kind touch. He'd been tamed. She was his light, the beam of hope to his existence. Tala was everything. Love was overflowing and the word seemed a pale description of how his heart cherished her.

He wanted her so much, to be a part of her, to give of himself, to share their lives in a bond of blood and trust. His soul cried for—he needed to have her, to claim her.

The need to feed ate at him. He wanted to drink from her, fill himself with her essence. He needed to give his entire being to her. Mist encircled him in a warm, welcoming embrace, encouraging him to love and mate.

His body burned to join with hers. She was so willing and open to him, he could take her right there. He wanted to mark her, feast upon her rich blood, tasting her upon his tongue. The need to make love to her, to join with her and claim her body and soul in a mating ritual, became a powerful driving force. Yet he refused to take her before it was time.

"Act, my friend. Show her your love. Make her your eternal mate. It is time," the mist seemed to whisper.

As Tala became more insistent, Lucius could sense her struggling to hold the beast at bay, refusing to let go of restraint.

He pulled up the hem of her dress as her body continued to writhe in want. By the gods, she was bare beneath her dress. No fabric to bar his way.

Animal instinct took over. The fangs grew within his mouth in anticipation of sinking into her. He could already taste her upon his tongue, her sweet, salty blood. It was like ambrosia from the gods, and all his.

He fumbled with his pants and released his cock, straining and hard, ready for action. In one swift stroke, he plunged into her slick core. She climaxed immediately, milking him with each squeeze.

"Take her. She is your mate," the mist whispered again.

Her screams of ecstasy drove him over the edge. His seed spilled into her, and he sunk his teeth into her shoulder. One gulp, then another, but he needed something more. They weren't complete. They had to fulfill their destiny.

Still trembling with his orgasm, he pulled away and bared his neck to her. She bit him. And drank. Her mouth closed over his neck and warmth shot through him. She drank hungrily, and he gave each drop with relish. Each sip a climactic high. By the gods, he wanted to give his all to her.

Yes, completion at last. She was his. They shared the blood bond.

She broke the contact and gasped for air. Lucius sensed the beast easing back before Tala gained control once again.

Then Lucius became conscious of his surroundings. He had mated with Tala in front of strangers. He looked up to find they had all left. Only he and Tala remained in the room. The candles flickered in the silence, strange after the endless music and singing.

But now they had to wait. Would Tala go insane? Did the ceremony rid them of the curse?

Only time would tell.

They lay in each other's arms amid the candlelight, reluctant to leave the comforting embrace of the dim silence.

"How long should we stay?" Tala asked in a sleepy voice.

"We could probably go now." He hesitated. "How do you feel?"

"Tired, but good. I feel…complete." Her face beamed.

The weight lifted from his heart. So far, so good. "Will you come with me to my resting place?"

"Yes, let's go. I'm so tired."

He rose then lifted her into his arms. "Seems I'm always carrying you around."

"So romantic. It's right out of one of my books."

"And how do I compare to one of your heroes?"

"Better than any author could create." She planted a kiss on his jaw and nestled into his neck. "I love you so much. I just want to sleep a thousand years in your arms."

"That's not all I want to do with you in my arms." He laughed soft and low. It vibrated through his chest.

She giggled. "You're bad."

"I told you, you don't know how bad I can really be."

"Yeah, well—I can be bad too."

Chapter Eight

That night, they retired into his stone tomb. Unlike what Tala had expected, the room had a homey interior. Black silk sheets covered a mattress. Thank goodness, no coffin!

Candles dimly lit the room, casting a warm glow over Lucius' handsome features. And he apparently conjured his clothes, for they disappeared the moment he lounged upon the mattress, a sheet pulled loosely up to his groin. Naked, he looked like sin incarnate, his white-blond hair a stark contrast to the dark sheets. His muscles, all sinew, beckoned to be touched. She itched to run her hands over each inch of his body.

A renewed energy filled Tala as she stepped toward the bed. Right now, she wanted to show him her passion. For once, she wanted to dominate this powerful vampire.

She pulled her dress over her head, baring her body to him.

"I noticed no panties earlier. Nor a bra." He chuckled. "Oh, you are bad."

Tala traced her curves with her fingertips, noting his gaze following each movement. "I wanted to be ready in case we decided to act on our animalistic impulses." She pinched her already-taut nipples.

He moaned. "Damn, woman. You're going to kill me by doing that."

"You want me to stop?" Her voice was seductive, fluid as she stepped onto the bed.

"Hell, no."

"Feeling frisky?"

"What do you have in mind?"

"I wanna taste you…then I wanna fuck you."

He growled low in his throat. "Talking naughty too. Oh, you are a bad girl tonight."

"I'm feeling wonderful. I think we beat the curse."

His face suddenly fell serious. "Think so?"

"I think so. I hope so."

"We'll know soon."

"Until then, I wanna love you, explore you. I just can't seem to get enough."

"Sounds like torture."

She pulled the sheet away, uncovering his erect penis, large and pulsing with life. He was hot for her already. Damn, it looked like satin-covered steel, and she caressed it between her palms.

Lucius moaned in answer to her touch.

"Like that, eh?" she couldn't help but tease.

He lay against the pillows, his eyes closed and his breathing rapid, already under the spell of her touch.

"I love the taste of you upon my tongue," she said, swiping it across the engorged head of his cock.

He groaned and ran his fingers through her hair, silently urging her to continue.

"Oh yes, you taste so wonderful, salty and addictive." She enclosed his cock in her mouth, taking him deep and sucking hard. Power over this vampire, immense authority over his entire being, felt incredible. She needed to bring him to his knees more often, weakening him to her, taking his trust and love as he surrendered control.

She increased the tempo of her ministrations, savoring the feel of him against her tongue.

He pushed her away. To her questioning glance, he breathed in a raspy voice, "I want you to ride me, Tala. Take me into you."

Crawling up his body, she relished the feel of her taut nipples gliding along his smooth skin. When she poised above his cock, he rested his hands on her hips. The head of his penis slid through the wet folds of her cleft, covering his shaft in her natural lubrication.

Tala slammed down over him, taking him into her to the hilt. She screamed at the immediate pleasure. He filled her body, completing her. She retreated then roughly took him in again.

He palmed her breasts, teasing her hard nipples into straining points of pleasure. Again and again, she took him into her. She needed him to go deeper, harder, to touch her inner being, her inner core. She needed to have all of him at her mercy.

Her thrusts became barely controlled bouncing as she rode his cock with wild, unbridled desire. When her body reacted to the sensual onslaught of their joining, she plunged over the edge and came. She felt like she flew through the air as her body's spasms closed and released around him.

He filled her with his cock and his essence while meeting her at the brink of ecstasy, the pinnacle of passion.

With her strength spent, she lay across his body, catching her breath. Each time they mated, it felt more amazing than the time before. And she'd have an eternity to love him.

Or would she?

She rolled to his side, and he gathered her into his embrace. In the still of the night, he rocked her body in a gentle sway.

Fatigue hit her. Tala eased down to sleep in the arms of her mate, hoping the morning would bring promise for their future.

* * * * *

Lucius caressed her in her sleep, enjoying the simple warmth of her body close to his. He longed to protect her, treasure her. At the approach of dawn, he'd know if the ritual had been successful.

Being an ancient of his kind, he could tolerate moving about during the daytime as long as he stayed out of the sun's direct rays. There within the tomb, they were both safe.

Even without seeing the sunrise, he would know when it arrived. And it would be hours from now. Until then, he'd hold her as she slept.

* * * * *

The sun began to peak on the horizon, and Lucius felt fatigue settle through his body. Tala still slept, and he was reluctant to wake her.

Then her eyelids snapped open. Violent shaking racked her body. "Dear God, what's happening?" She sounded panicky, and instantaneous fear filled her eyes.

All Lucius could do was hold her and try to ease the pain. As her body convulsed beneath his, she was beyond his touch.

"Tell her of your love," a misty voice whispered in his ears. The voice from last night—the invoked spirit that was to protect them.

Sitting up in bed, he cradled Tala in his arms, rocking her back and forth. This wasn't over yet, he realized, stroking her head, now drenched with sweat. This was the trial moment.

"Tala, love, fight for your life. Fight for us. I want to love you forever. Don't leave me to long for you alone like Damon longs for your sister. Stay with me."

Still, her body spasmed. She seemed out of reach as the curse coursed through her body, killing her before his eyes.

"If you leave me, I'll meet the sun and join you on the other side, Tala. I can't exist without you. I waited too long to love you." Anger at her obvious surrender to the power coursing through her body and soul brimmed to the surface. "I refuse to let you go! Damn it, fight!"

Her body stilled and fell limp in his arms, as though she had lost all her strength.

Her heart ceased.

Lucius screamed in rage. He had lost her!

And for the first time since his turning, tears escaped his eyes, and the vampire cried over the body of his mate.

* * * * *

Darkness engulfed her, surrounded her, and she couldn't move. She became vaguely aware of Lucius holding her. His pain echoed within the darkness, calling her back to him.

The call of a phantom pack in the distance, however, was drawing her to them. She could run with them and be a part of their group. She'd never be lonely again. Never want for company or…

Love?

No, she had left her mate behind. She couldn't leave him, her lover and friend. The other half to her entire being.

The pack again called to her, and she felt her body shift form. She loped up to the pack and recognized one dark gray wolf—Telia.

The others, mainly males, nuzzled her body. Their ghostly forms sent tingles of odd sensations through her, unlike touching the coat of Lucius in his wolfish form.

Telia trotted forward with a bigger black wolf. They howled and called for Tala to follow. Running with the pack felt exhilarating, never had she felt this free…

Or had she?

In Lucius' arms, she had felt a certain freedom. Lucius. Her mate. She longed for him. How could she choose to run with the phantom pack and leave her love behind to suffer?

Telia and the black leader led the pack through a ghostly forest. No, this wasn't right. Tala didn't belong here. This wasn't her place.

Then abruptly, Telia stopped, and the entire pack halted. Telia padded over to her sister. "You're right. It's not time for you to join us. Go back to your lover, back to earth."

"How could you have left Damon? Did you have a choice?"

"Damon suffers, but his destiny didn't lie with me." Telia turned her head toward the black wolf then glanced back at Tala. "There is another for Damon. Tell him…" Telia paused. "Tell him to never lose hope. I will always be with him until he finds love once again."

The pack now barked in excitement.

"Now, go back, sister. We will run together someday, but you have a destiny of eternal love yet to fulfill."

Tala stood motionless as she watched the pack leader caress Telia. They led the pack into a shaft of light then disappeared.

Lucius' voice broke the silence surrounding her. "Come back to me."

Her heart filled with love for her mate, and that power drew her through the darkness, back into her mortal form.

And back to Lucius.

She gasped a large breath.

His tears of joy greeted her as he rained kisses over her face. "Damn it, what took you so long?" he asked through his celebration.

"Didn't you ever hear that patience is a virtue?"

"I have no patience, woman. Don't ever scare me like that again."

"There won't be a need. I'll never leave you again."

* * * * *

That evening, Lucius and Tala visited the Devil's Talon, where Monique and the others warmly greeted them.

"I see things worked out well," Monique quipped.

"Thanks to you," Tala said as she reached out to the other woman.

Monique squeezed the neophyte vampire's hand. "No, it was the strength of your love for each other that broke the curse."

"I was afraid for a while that I had lost her." Lucius looked disturbed to admit his weakness.

"So what are you?" Leonardo asked Tala. "A werewolf vampire?"

"I guess so." Tala absolutely beamed with the glow of a woman in love.

Some vampires have all the luck, Leo thought. "Anyone see Titania tonight? She hasn't been around the past two nights."

"Yeah, noticed that," Raife said. "Any idea why?"

"Not sure. But I have a bad feeling about it." Leo had a bond to her, having exchanged blood in the past. And they'd been lovers when he first came to New Orleans, so he knew her fairly well. Staying away from her friends was unlike her.

"So, Lucius, you going to change your ways because of love?" Alonso teased, obviously feeling bold enough to take on the love-struck vamp.

"Just as many changes as you went through when you met Jolie." With a cocked blond brow, Lucius added, "Watch yourself, young one. I know all your deepest secrets to get you in trouble with your mate."

"Oh, like you don't have any?"

"All right, you two. Enough." Jolie nipped playfully at Alonso's neck.

"Oh, Christ, no!"

Titania's voice ripped through Leo's brain. Scared. No—petrified. Fearful for her very life.

Leo shot up, ignoring the questioning looks from his friends. He rushed through the crowd and out the door. From there, he used his ethereal speed and followed her calls of pain and torture through the streets of New Orleans.

A sharp pain radiated through his chest, and he felt Titania give up to scorching agony.

What the hell was happening to her?

* * * * *

Down a dark side alley off Bourbon Street, Leo found Titania lying on the cold cobblestone. Over her stood a woman with long red hair and a fair complexion.

Then Leonardo saw it—Titania's headless body, a wooden stake protruding from its chest. This human woman had just murdered his friend.

A vampire slayer? Here?

The woman gazed up. Her emerald green eyes struck him, pinning him to the spot.

Anger bubbled to the surface. He approached, cautiously noting she had another stake in one hand.

"Who the hell are you?" he asked, rage spouting from his every pore.

"Your worst nightmare, vampire."

Chapter Nine

Leonardo

"Oh, Christ, no!" the female vampire frantically pleaded, tears streaming down her face.

"God isn't here to help you," vampire slayer Erin O'Connell sneered. She shoved the vampire's weakened body against the brick wall of the building beside the alley then twisted the stake protruding from her chest.

The wet, cool surface of the wall matched the vampire's own temperature, which was rapidly losing heat. Dark, rich blood oozed from the massive chest wound. Without feeding, the vampire would become incapacitated as her precious life fluid pumped from her body.

The ancient belief of a stake through the heart was still the most effective way to impair a vampire. Only decapitation would ensure the final death, or the greeting of the morning sun, incinerating the remains into ash to be scattered with the wind.

The vampire lost consciousness and slid down the wall into a heap.

Erin had no time to wait hours for the sun. She pulled a machete from an inner pocket of her long trench coat, the polished blade gleaming in the soft streetlight. What a beautiful piece of equipment for such a dreadful task. But it wasn't anything new to her. This vampire marked her fifty-first kill.

Raising her arm, feeling the weight of the weapon, Erin let all her inner hate and passion for revenge bubble up through her. With a scowl, she swung the blade and severed the head from the vampire's body.

She had been a slayer ever since that one horrible night eight years ago when a male vampire had eased his way into her parents' home by dating her older sister, Karen.

Karen had talked constantly about Michael, a dark, handsome man she had met in the university library. She had thought he was a student, but it turned out Michael was a three-hundred-year-old vampire. Before their eyes, he had changed from a charming man into a bloodthirsty demon.

He fed upon Erin's family, enslaving them under his magic spell as he drank from each at his leisure. When he had gotten to Erin, however, a vampire slayer interrupted him.

The slayer, Casey, a twenty-five-year-old man with dark hair and eyes and a muscular build, had been delayed by one of the vampire's minions. He arrived in time only to save Erin from being drained. Unfortunately, Michael had escaped after the ensuing battle.

From that moment, Erin vowed to find the demon that destroyed her family, and all those who shared his fate. Casey had taken her under his wing for two years, teaching her the art of slaying.

Convincing him to allow her to become involved in such a dangerous business had proven difficult at first, but he eventually relented. At nineteen, Erin began to learn how to hunt and kill vampires.

After a year with Casey, Erin began to care for him, wishing she could give in to her inner desires. He, however, had been secretly in love with Karen. Teaching Erin the ways of the slayer had been his way of avenging Karen's death. When Erin eventually discovered the truth, she left Casey to continue her work alone. It hurt too much to see the man she adored yearning for her dead sister, so Erin immersed herself in her work to ease the pain racking her heart.

In six years on her own as a slayer, she had sent fifty vampires to their eternal rest. She moved about the United States, all the while following Michael's movements. His hunting grounds became hers. He sought victims, meals for the evening, while she tracked him and those of his kind.

Then, three months ago, Michael disappeared. He had never gone to ground before, but she had begun to believe that he had done so.

One recent night, however, she came face to face with him in the streets of Philadelphia. He had just fed off a hooker in a back alley. Erin confronted him, and it became her most difficult skirmish. She got in a blow that severed his jugular, causing him to run off into the night faster than she could follow. She hadn't seen him since.

Three days ago, she decided to visit the American vampire capital, New Orleans. She could almost sense the evil about her, and amid it, Michael, the damned night-walker who had destroyed everyone she held dear.

But where was he?

It was while searching for clues to Michael's whereabouts that Erin had run into this female vampire. She tried to persuade the one called Titania to introduce her to the city's vampire society. Titania, of course, was apprehensive. Erin tried weakening her with a special potion Casey had created that could drain some of a vampire's strength. Still, Titania would not willingly reveal the secret gathering places of her fellow demons, so Erin had had no other choice but to kill her.

Now, in the alley off Bourbon Street, darkness surrounded her as she stood over the corpse. Not a pretty sight. A grueling, messy job, but someone had to do it. And this one had been tough—but again, Erin had triumphed.

A male vampire, still hidden by shadows, burst onto the scene. Erin could feel his anger as he gazed over the staked, headless body.

"Who the hell are you?" he asked, rage spouting from his every pore.

"Your worst nightmare, vampire."

Obviously, these two creatures had had a connection, bringing him to her with her pained call for help. Perfect. Now Erin could destroy two of them, making it a very productive evening.

He stepped from the shadows, revealing his handsome features in the dim street light. Erin gasped. His chiseled jaw, dark eyes and short black hair—matched with a tall stature—made her heart leap. A skintight T-shirt prominently displayed his well-toned chest and a washboard abdomen, and his lean, muscular legs were encased in body hugging blue jeans. It was hard to breathe, as though all air had escaped her lungs. Lust shot through her body, betraying each and every instinct she had honed in the past eight years.

For the first time in all her years as a hunter, she felt confused. How could her body react in such a way to one of the night-walkers? She had trained to kill them, no matter her feelings. But somehow, she couldn't lift the machete to strike out at him.

"Who are you?" she whispered.

"The one about to destroy you. Damn you, slayer!" He approached with ethereal speed, knocking her to the cobblestones. The machete flew out of her hand and into the dark shadows.

His hard, muscled body pressed her down onto the equally hard alley. Erin struggled for release, but he securely held her wrists on each side of her head. She gazed into his face and gasped again. He appeared even more striking when closer. Moisture pooled between her legs as her traitorous body awakened with desires long denied.

He hovered above her, those chocolate-brown eyes intense with hate. Yet for a moment, a flash of something else reflected in those dark mirrors to his soul. Had it been her imagination, or had she seen a spark of lust?

His body could not hide its reaction to her. She felt the telltale sign of his arousal pressing into her pubis. She eased open her legs, and he nestled his bulging erection close to her core. She moaned as the sensations triggered her body to urge along his contact.

She wanted him, needed to feel connected to him, this vampire, one of the creatures for which she had spent part of her life hunting. Damn, what a confusing situation.

"Will you kill me now?" she croaked in a small voice.

He continued to stare into her eyes. A bevy of emotions and expressions flashed across his face, as though he couldn't decide what her fate would be at his hands. He surprised her by lowering his lips above hers. "Perhaps there is some other way to exact my vengeance." He covered her lips in a bruising, possessive kiss.

Erin's entire being responded to the awakened passion. His tongue probed her mouth in a sensual assault, tasting her in sure strokes. Her body arched beneath his powerful mastery over her senses. His hard body answered the silent pleas of her own by pressing firmly between her legs. For a moment, she thought he'd take her there in the alley amid the nearby gore of her latest hunt.

That last thought slammed her back to her senses. She had vowed to track and kill the dreaded vampires, vile creatures that lived off the blood and lives of humans. This one was no different, no matter his allure.

She struggled against his kisses and embrace, refusing to submit to the intoxicating caresses. She would not let the enemy into her life other than in the role of "the hunted".

When the kiss ended, the vampire once again stared into her face. He growled and leapt off her body. In a flash of speed, he collected the remains of the female vampire and dashed off into the night, leaving behind only the dark redness pooling over the ancient cobblestones.

Erin rose from the damp ground just as the sky opened up and rain began to pelt her. She continued to stand within the sudden storm and watched the blood wash into oblivion.

Quickly drenched to the bone, her hair matted to her body, she snatched her lost machete and placed it inside her long coat. No words would come to her. She had killed a vampire and met another that affected her like no other male—human or otherwise. As she walked home, she couldn't help but wonder if she'd ever see him again.

* * * * *

Leonardo laid Titania's remains upon the roof of her resting tomb in St. Louis Cemetery. Many of his fellow beings had tombs in the historic cemetery. Luckily, the heavy stone doors kept them fairly safe from most humans, while rumors of ghosts and vampires kept the curious from finding out the truth. Fear acted as the main weapon for survival.

He placed a sheet over the battered body, knowing Titania would rather be remembered for her beauty than her means of destruction. There upon the roof, her remains would greet the morning sun, burn away to ash and scatter in the winds. Vampires did not rebury their fallen. What was the sense? No, the body was only a vessel for the soul. Cremation via sunlight was the way to ensure the soul found eternal rest.

"I heard what happened." In mid-shift from the form of a gray owl, Raife landed on the neighboring tomb's roof. "Any idea how Ti met a slayer?"

"No, and we may never know."

Leonardo looked up at the blond vampire, who had been his friend since they met in England back in 1600.

At the time, Raife had been a privateer for Elizabeth I, and questions began to rise as to why he didn't age while his queen deteriorated. Leonardo had met him in a house of ill repute, drinking from one of the ladies of the night. Lenoardo took the fledgling Raife under his care and taught him the finer points of vampiric life. They eventually left England and traveled to the Americas. As the years rolled by, they considered themselves Americans and had sided with the rebels when the Revolution began.

After the Americans won their independence, Raife wished to return to England for a visit. He told Leo the story of his sweetheart, a vampire who, consequently, made him one as well. She had turned him during a night of debauchery while he celebrated a British victory over the Spanish Armada. He had been angry with her for a long time yet wished to remain with the woman whom he'd never stopped loving. As time passed, however, he discovered her true nature—that of an evil vampire, without any remorse for her actions. Raife was heartbroken and existed with the knowledge that the woman he once loved was a *demoni scuri*.

While Raife and Leo were in England, the residents of Whitechapel were amid panic with a gruesome killer on the loose—the Ripper. The man left his victims in such a horrid state—only a man in possession of a truly deranged mind could have performed such crimes. Of course, the vampire community knew the truth—Jack had been a vampire, the worst of their kind. Unfortunately, he disappeared from the scene before the police caught him and solved the mystery. Leonardo and Raife both agreed the demon had gone to ground to seek his rest. He would emerge once again someday.

Afterward, they traveled to Leonardo's home in Florence, Italy, where they stayed until World War I broke. At that time, they chose to return to America, having already fought in too many of the human battles. They arrived in New Orleans and had been there since.

In all his time as a vampire, having been transformed during the Italian High Renaissance, Leonardo had never met a woman to take away the pain of his loneliness. He had relieved his physical urges with numerous women, but none ever stood apart from the rest.

That was what made the encounter with the slayer this evening that much more disturbing. As soon as he had touched her, he felt the connection. There was no other explanation—she was his life-mate. But after waiting hundreds of years, why did she have to be his enemy?

Her image haunted him. Her softness and scent intoxicated his senses. She had yielded beneath him, as though instinct had taken over. Her body fit to his to perfection, and he grew hard at the thought of her naked, giving in to her desire to bond with him.

Her long, dark auburn hair would flow freely about her shoulders and fan along the pillow as her body arched upward in anticipation of his touch. He could already imagine her creamy white skin glowing in the moonlight as he bent to taste her erect nipple. He already knew it would taste sweeter than any berry, and his mouth watered to sample its texture against his tongue. He had smelled her womanly arousal, and the scent permeated him. Her nectar would be a delicious treat before he eventually drank her rich blood, combining their souls for all eternity. Yes, the thought of her drinking from him aroused him more than he'd ever dreamed possible.

"Leo, what's wrong?" Raife interrupted his thoughts.

"It's the slayer. I can't get her off my mind."

"We need to avenge Ti's death. Why didn't you kill her?"

"I just couldn't."

"But why?"

"She's the one…the one I've been waiting for."

Raife growled. "She cannot live after destroying our own. She must be punished. You know the rules."

"I'll see to it that she's punished for her crimes. I promise you that—but only I will deal with her." Leo glanced up into the angry face of his longtime friend. "Don't touch her, understand?"

Raife nodded in silence as his eyes grazed Titania's still figure. "We must seek our rest for now. The sun approaches." Raife shifted once again into an owl and flew off to his own resting place.

Leonardo's troubled mind would not let him rest easily. He jumped down from the tomb and wandered through the cemetery as others of his kind sought their rest.

Loneliness crashed into Leo's soul as he thought of those who had found their mates. Never had he dreamed a *demoni* like Lucius would fall under the spell of eternal love and devotion. So much had changed in a few days.

Stopping by the tomb of Marie Laveau, Leonardo examined the Xs that decorated the ancient stone. Humans believed in the Voodoo Queen and her magic that helped those in need. Perhaps he should ask for help. It wasn't every day he found his life-mate, but for her to be a slayer as well—it was a deep problem not easily solved.

"How am I to proceed?" he asked aloud, placing a hand against the cool tomb wall. "She is destined to be my mate, but will she love me—or kill me?"

The stone vibrated in response beneath his fingertips.

Chapter Ten

Erin stretched her aching muscles while she lay in bed. She had fallen asleep as soon as her head hit the soft pillow that morning. Glancing at the clock, she realized she had slept away most of the day. It was already three in the afternoon.

It wasn't as though she had rested easily. Images of the vampire that tackled her to the ground filled her mind. By God, he was everything sexy and desirable. She had always thought Casey was her dream man, but he couldn't compare to the dark, handsome vampire from last night.

Her body had hummed beneath his touch, and when he kissed her—no, it wasn't a kiss. He had marked her with that meeting of mouths.

Trying to ignore the disturbing thoughts of his effect on her senses, she climbed out of bed and took a quick shower. After dressing, she made coffee. As she sipped the dark, bitter brew, she couldn't get the memory of the vampire's body covering hers from her mind.

This would not be tolerated. She couldn't let a man—a vampire, of all things—deter her from her duties. The problem had only one answer—the vampire had to be destroyed.

But how would she find him?

Then again, if he felt the same powerful attraction as she, he would find her.

Erin smiled. Yes, he would search for her—and she would be ready.

After gulping down the last of her coffee, she set the cup in the sink and proceeded to gather the tools she'd need for her trap.

The vampire would likely come for her tonight, and she'd use herself as bait. She checked her coat for all her supplies—four wooden stakes, her weakening potion mixed in pig's blood, holy water and her trusty machete. Everything was there, ready for use.

She didn't bother with things like mirrors, garlic or crosses. Garlic irritated a vampire, as well as humans. You didn't attract anyone with garlic in your pocket. Mirrors were of no use—it was a silly superstition that vampires do not reflect. They were solid beings, therefore they had a reflection. And crosses were only as powerful as the beliefs of their owners. Watching her entire family get brutally murdered by a vampire who was still on the loose had eaten away at any belief Erin may have had in divine justice.

Now she had to plan the place of the upcoming confrontation. Graveyards were out of the question, being the worst places to confront a vampire. You never knew when more night-walkers would show up to join in the battle.

Where would be a good place for her to set her trap?

As she touched the clean blade of her machete, the answer hit her—the rooftop of her apartment building. The flat-top roof, high above the city and away from innocent lives, would be a perfect place to confront the vampire. She knew every crack and crevice—everything—and where better than to confront him than on her own turf? True, a meeting on a rooftop was risky, but it was better than having someone stumble upon a battle taking place in an alley. She wanted low resistance from outside sources. And risks were part of the job—there was no quick getaway from an immortal vampire. Running away was never an option.

Glancing at her watch, she saw it was almost five o'clock. If she hurried, she could get to the roof before darkness fell and the vampire had risen from his rest. When he came to her—and he *would* come to her—she'd be waiting.

* * * * *

Leonardo rose from his tomb in the St. Louis Cemetery. Sniffing the air, he could sense the slayer, smelling her sweet perfume upon the wind. It was a combination of herbal shampoo, body lotion and her unique scent. Did he truly smell her, or was it remnants of the night before when he had crushed her body beneath his? That was something he wanted to do again—and soon.

Attraction to any human was almost foreign to him. Since he'd become a vampire all those years ago, he had touched only one human woman in lust or desire. That had been a disaster.

It had happened just after he had been turned at the hands of another vampire wearing the guise of an angel. The creature had changed Leo into a *demoni* before he even realized what had happened. The vampire thrust him over to this existence then left him to die in a Roman alley, drained of blood and substance.

His creator did not wait around and instruct Leo in the vampiric ways but left him to his own volition. That was what had probably drawn him to Raife years later, who had been left the same way—hungry, alone and scared.

The human woman, a simple servant, had attracted him. He had watched her during his humanity, passing her in the marketplace while he ran errands for his master, Michelangelo. Later he found out she served his master's rival, Raphael. Not wanting to endanger his artistic dreams of learning the ways of fresco painting, Leo never touched her—until he turned into a night creature.

The hunger within him clawed and fought to be sated by none other than the sweet girl. He approached her and coaxed her to his side, using his powers of persuasion and animal magnetism. She came willingly, reeking of sexual excitement and curiosity.

He took her that night, easing the hunger raging within. He became rough and very much the *demoni*. Her sweet virginal blood tasted like wine over his tongue, and plunging into her tight sheath undid his last hold on control. He ceased his ferocious treatment of her in the nick of time, sending her into a deep sleep before taking her home. If he hadn't come to his senses when he did, he would have killed her. Since then, Leo had promised never to become involved with a human woman again.

He'd sip from them, but he never took it further. Coupling the hunger with sexual pleasure made it difficult to control the consequences. He refused to hurt another female. Controlling his lust and desire along with his need to feed would be just too much for him to guarantee the safety of the woman involved.

Hunger for the female slayer, however, grew overbearing. He wanted to taste her, feast upon her blood and body in a sexual mating. He needed to make the slayer his for all eternity.

But how could he do that without confronting her anger? She killed his kind for a living, and turning her would be difficult. Was there any way to make her his ally instead of his enemy?

Darkness covered the cemetery, and he stood watching the vampire community rise from its rest. Alonso and Jolie left their tomb amid small embraces and stolen kisses. Alonso playfully nipped the tender flesh at her neck, and she laughed in complete delight.

Jealousy coursed through Leo's every fiber. He wanted to have a loving relationship with his mate. He just didn't know how he could ever get the tempting vampire hunter to fall in love with him.

"Leo?" a familiar male voice asked from behind.

Leo turned to gaze into Raife's concerned face. "I'm sorry. Once we feed, I have to meet up with the slayer."

"Sure you don't need help?"

"No, but if I do, I'll call."

"How are you going to make her pay for her deeds?"

Leo gazed into the distance toward the city and said soulfully, "I'll make her one of us."

* * * * *

Erin waited in readiness to confront the sexy, dark vampire. She had to hold firm to her beliefs—vampires were evil and must be destroyed. She gripped the handle of her machete. It felt comforting as she awaited the confrontation. If she acted quickly, she'd have no time to reflect on how his deep brown eyes gazed upon her, sending shivers of excitement through her body. Maybe she could ignore the moisture gathering between her legs and end the creature's existence without yearning for him to fill her to the core, pounding into her body with a relentless tempo, marking her as his own.

Damn it. Thoughts like these were dangerous and completely unlike her. So much for being unaffected. Her body already hummed with anticipation for his touch.

The slightest movement in the darkness caught her attention.

"What is your name, *mia* slayer *dolce*, my sweet slayer?" His voice broke through the night, cutting into her heart already longing for his love.

Shit. Did she just think the word "love"? Where the hell did that come from? "Erin," she said, annoyed with herself.

"Erin, the Irish lass who captured my heart the moment I laid eyes upon her beauty," he said as he stepped into the pale moonlight. His features were as handsome as she remembered. He exuded male charm and charisma, and Erin found her purpose tonight wane into oblivion.

"I can't get involved with you… Who are you?" Her voice wavered as he stepped closer. His scent of spice intoxicated her senses. No man had the right to smell so wonderful.

"Leonardo, *mia amore*. I know you have your reasons for what you do, but what I feel right now transcends all reason. I have searched for hundreds of years for the one woman—my life-mate."

He stood inches away from her body. Even without touching him, Erin could feel the heat from his body searing into her own. She thought if she did touch him, her fingers would surely burn.

"Life-mate?" she whispered, trying to keep her senses. He was just too seductive in his movements and enticing in his voice.

"*Si*, Erin, you are my life-mate, *mia compagna di vita*."

Oh, Lord, she had always been a sucker for a man with an accent. An Italian accent, at that.

She released her machete and it fell to the rooftop with a clank. He was too powerful. His seduction too hypnotic. She laid a hand on his chest, feeling it rise and fall beneath her fingers. He was hot and so real, so tempting. She should listen to her inner voice. What was it saying?

All thoughts left her mind as he laid his hands on her shoulders, pulling her to him. Fire shot through her body at the points of contact with his.

"*Il mia* slayer *dolce del mia cuore*—my sweet slayer of my heart, let me kiss you," he whispered.

All her resolve and doubts melted away as their lips joined in a tender kiss. Nothing so gentle could be evil, could it?

The pace quickened to a feverish urgency as she clutched his body, opening her lips for him to taste her, sample her. His tongue plunged into her mouth, dancing with hers, drinking in her essence.

A small moan caught in her throat, a surprise even to her. She was being swept away by desire and passion for a vampire. And she didn't care. Years of hatred and hunting had become lost with the touch of his lips, the brush of his tongue, the caress of his fingertips.

Oh, the sensation! He deepened the kiss as his hands explored her body, molding her form to his lean, hard one. She fit perfectly with him, her soft curves a perfect match to his muscled carriage.

Her hands became hungry for more, wanting to feel flesh next to her own. Clothes became a barrier, a nuisance, a wall between her and the man assaulting her mouth with his tongue.

When his fingertips traced the curve of her breast, she thought she'd fall apart in his arms. He cupped it in his hand, making her groan. Pinching the nipple, already hard and erect, straining against the constraining fabric of her bra, he blew apart all resistance.

Damn it, she needed to have him inside her. Now!

Tugging at his clothes, not breaking the contact of their mouths and tongues, instinct took over and she peeled away the barriers. He did the same.

Her trench coat landed in a heap at her feet, thudding from all the weapons concealed within. Her pants and shirt and the scraps of undergarments followed. As he stripped her, she pulled off his shirt, baring the sculpted muscles and bronze skin. Running hungry hands over its hardness, she memorized his body, mapping her way with each caress.

After she unfastened his pants and pushed them down, his penis stood large and full from the dark nest at his groin. By God, she never thought anything could look so wonderful, so tantalizing. Her mouth watered to taste the engorged head and the small droplet forming upon it.

She dropped to her knees and faced the masterpiece of male anatomy then gingerly touched it with her fingertips. He moaned as she stroked its length with her fingers. His stance wavered, and when she looked up, his eyes closed and he tossed back his head, absorbed in the sensations she created. Such power over a man felt intoxicating.

She touched the droplet of pre-come with the tip of her tongue. Relishing the salty taste, she covered the swollen head with her full lips, massaging the pleasure point with delicate strokes. He moaned and dipped his fingers into her thick hair, urging her to continue her sensual assault.

Sucking at his length, Erin lost all notion of time. He tasted wonderful, and his groans encouraged her to suck harder. She felt in control, completely in ecstasy in pleasuring this handsome male.

Her hands traveled over the sculpted muscles of his thighs and his ass. Magnificent. She squeezed his cheeks, drawing him farther into her mouth, and he moaned as she took him deeper.

Finally, he grunted and pushed her away. Erin licked her lips as he gazed down at her face.

With a husky voice, he said, "You'll make me come before I have a chance to give you pleasure, *mia dolce*. I want our joining to be relished and enjoyed by both of us. I don't view you for my pleasure only. I want to give as well as receive."

"Leo, I don't think I can be patient enough right now. I need you inside me," she said, lying back, their discarded clothes padding her body from the rooftop. Propping herself up on her elbows, she smiled seductively and opened her legs for him to gaze upon her moist slit.

She knew how she looked, the temptress exposing her core to his gaze. Her pussy was wet, weeping for his touch. Even her clit throbbed—just the slightest attention would send her over the edge. She could feel her labia part to expose her slit more to him, communicating her desires in her scent and actions. Teasingly, she parted her legs then closed them, tempting him to attack her body.

But he's a vampire!

Her inner voice pleaded with her, the trained sensibility attempting to reason with her desires. It would not work. To have his cock deep inside her sheath, pounding into her heated core—the thoughts made cream form around her opening. All reason fled as she poised to mate with him.

"You don't want me to take it slow?" he asked, bringing her attention back to his face instead of his proud cock.

"Fuck me, honey. I just want you to fuck me like you hadn't had a good fuck in centuries."

He crouched down to her, balancing on the balls of his feet, his elbows resting on his thighs. "Oh, I'm going to fuck you, *mia amore*. I'll be the only one to have that pleasure for the rest of eternity." Before she could answer, he commanded, "Now, turn over onto your stomach. Lift that luscious ass in the air and part your legs. I want to see that pussy beg my cock to fuck it into tomorrow."

Erin realized how much control she had, and liked it, but now she wanted him to have the power—dominance over her body and heart. Only Leo could make her intimate muscles clench with anticipation at this request. She turned over, leaning on her forearms and raising onto her knees. She spread her legs to allow him full view of her pussy. She'd trimmed the hair that afternoon while in the shower, even though she had denied her desires for him to touch her tonight. Perhaps a secret wish made her do it, but she was ready. Her juices flowed and her clit ached.

"Now, *mia* slayer *dolce*, I want you to touch yourself. Show me where you want me to touch you."

"Aren't you going to—"

"I said touch yourself—don't question it, just do it. Feel sexy as you perform for me, knowing I watch you bring yourself to ecstasy."

She gulped, unsure about this request. She wasn't used to taking orders, but somehow it excited her. Most of all, she'd never masturbated for anyone before, and the thought of doing it for this dark man more than excited, more than stimulated her. It felt climactic.

Leaning on one elbow, she brought her free arm beneath her and gasped when her fingertips brushed the swollen nubbin. She stroked her clit—slick with her juices—in slow passes. He growled, low and primal, and it encouraged her further to explore this new position. It seemed as if she held the power—by pleasing him, following his command.

As she stroked her clit, her vaginal muscles clenched. God, she just wanted him inside her, to grip that tasty cock while he held his hips tight against his groin.

She steadily climbed the precipice of arousal. Just when she thought she'd orgasm, she felt his fingertip trace her wet entrance. She whimpered as she climbed higher while his fingers slid through her wet folds, spreading the moisture up to the tight rosette of her anus. He paused there before sliding back down to her feminine opening. She thought she'd burst from his intimate caress.

He pulled away his fingers and she moaned in frustration. She wiggled her hips to tantalize him into returning his touch.

"Just like the finest Italian wine, sweet and delicious," he said. She heard him taste her juices from his fingertips.

Groaning once again, Erin ached to find release from the pleasurable torment. She needed him to plunge into her. When she heard him move behind her and felt the warm brush of his flesh against her backside, she jumped in anticipation. Then he took her hips between his hands and positioned his cock to enter her.

He paused, then said in a barely controlled voice, "Erin, *mia amore*, I'm going to fuck you now. I want you to come for me when I command it, not before. Do you understand?"

How could she hold back her body's reaction to his invasion? "Yes," she croaked, unsure if she'd be able to comply, especially with her body already at the breaking point.

"Putting off your orgasm will enhance the experience. If you come before I tell you, I'll have to punish you later."

She nodded in understanding.

He entered her, filling her slick passage to the hilt, giving her the missing part of her soul. She screamed and her body reacted, clenching around his cock, hugging it, inviting him to go in farther.

Tears burned her eyes as he began to move within her, thrusting into her sheath then retreating…thrust, then retreat…thrust, retreat. He slammed into her body, his balls knocking against her mound, juices running from her, lubricating his passageway to paradise. She met his thrusts by moving her hips, and their movements quickly escalated to a frenzied pace. His tempo increased along with his breathing. His grip on her hips became stronger as he guided his cock in and out of her canal. He moved one hand to press slightly into her anus with a finger, and she about lost control. She could feel her orgasm approach when he yelled to her, "Come now, Erin. Come for me."

She couldn't stop the climax that shuddered through her body, her vaginal walls squeezing his penis, milking him of his seed as he joined her over the edge of reason, past conscious thoughts and actions and into the land of blissful ecstasy. He called out her name with a howl, appropriate for the moment, as though announcing to the world his claim to her body and soul.

This vampire completed her in a way she never thought possible. How could such a connection occur so quickly and with such intensity?

As he eased out of her body and lay upon their discarded clothes, he pulled her down to rest in the curve of his arm. They spooned, chest to back, and his arms wrapped around her.

She sighed. Yes, this was the man for her. Yet he was a vampire. Why didn't he bite her? Why didn't he drink from her?

"We aren't all the same, *mia dolce,*" he said as if reading her mind. "There are different types of us just as there are different kinds of humans."

"What do you mean? Vampires are…" She just couldn't call him a beast. He wasn't, yet the thought went against the teachings she had learned since the day of her family's death.

"There are bad vampires and good ones. Ones who hunt and kill for their meals are the worst of our kind. Many of us do not follow such a lifestyle. Only a few have slipped to the dark side and become the terrors to all, including vampires."

She turned over in his arms so she could look at his face. He looked so handsome in the moonlight, dark skin with jet-black hair and sensual lips. His brown eyes could heat her with one look, melting her into a puddle of quivering flesh. "But I thought you'd bite me. Why didn't you?"

Tracing her cheek with his index finger, he said, "I was tempted. It's a battle not to, even now. All I'd like to do is sink my teeth into your soft skin and sip from your veins the fluid I long for." He paused. "I don't think that would be the right way for us to begin, forcing you to become what I wish you to be."

He wanted her to become as he…an immortal vampire? "But you commanded me to…to do things I've never done before."

Chuckling, he held her closer. "I ordered you to give your body pleasure. You followed my instructions by choice. Changing into a vampire is something I also wish for you to choose."

How could he even think of making her a vampire? "Never!"

She jumped from his arms and stood naked before him. Even now, she could feel her body betray her in reaction to his closeness. She'd just had sex with a vampire who wanted to make her one. Not while she could still fight. But her body still glowed from sexual satisfaction even though he was her enemy. Or was he her lover?

Leo snapped his attention from Erin to something in the darkness. Quickly, he shot up and threw Erin her clothes. "Get dressed, *mia amore*, we have visitors."

"Yes, Leo, you do indeed."

Chapter Eleven

Erin gasped as she pulled on her shirt. That voice sounded all too familiar.

"And look, Michael, he's got a new playmate," a female voice said, laughing from behind the dark figure.

"Michael, what the hell are you doing here…and with her?" Leo spat as he stepped into his jeans.

The new couple approached, and Erin's rage replaced her desire when she realized the creature that destroyed her family was standing before her.

She crouched on the rooftop and reached for her machete. There was no way she'd let this opportunity slide away. Leo knew her enemy, her long-sought prey? What was their connection?

"Oh, now, Leo, my brother, you didn't expect me to go through this existence alone, did you?"

"I told you a century ago never to call me brother again!" Leo said, fuming in his own rising anger. His entire body appeared rigid, on alert, like a cat poised for an upcoming attack. "You're no relative of mine anymore!"

Brother? Erin fought to keep her strength from failing. How could they be brothers? One was loving and kind, while the other was nothing but a monster! She rose silently, clutching the machete by her side and waiting behind Leo.

"But Leo, you are the only relative I have left. After all this time, we have only each other." Michael smiled, and his dark features took on a sinister aura. Evil permeated the air about him, while Leo radiated sexual appeal.

The beautiful, olive-skinned woman with mysterious dark eyes seemed strange to Erin, but she fit Michael's character. Her long black hair hung loose down her back. Dressed all in black, she could easily blend into the night as one of its creatures. When she smiled, she hissed. Her gaze slid up and down Erin, making the hairs on the back of her neck stand up. "Who is this little Patty?"

Erin felt more than tempted to slice the smirk off the woman's face.

"She is my mate," Leo said, placing himself between them. "Back off, bitch."

"Now, now, Leo, is that any way to talk to my mate?" Michael asked, placing a hand on the woman's shoulder and stilling her advance.

"Eva is bad news, Michael, and you know it. She turns men into monsters then leaves them to fend for themselves, unaware of the changes to come."

The woman laughed. "Poor little Raife. You have been protective of my former playmate for centuries. He was a big boy and has done well."

"You left him hungry and scared. Not only that—you hurt him deeply."

"Perhaps I should renew my suit for his heart and watch him fall for me all over again," Eva taunted.

"I have to say, Leo, I'm surprised you were able to get into the slayer's panties," Michael said, looking at Erin with an intense glare. "She's been chasing me for years after I had a wonderful feast with her family. She wants to kill me so badly, she can taste it. She hates us, Leo. All of us. I've seen how she slaughters us. She is not one to mate with, brother. Fuck her if you must, but then kill her. She'll only slice off your head one day when she realizes what you really are."

"You fucker! You don't deserve to live!" Erin spat. If she got close enough, she would indeed end his existence, severing his head from his body, killing the devil she had chased all these years. Leo wrapped an arm about her waist, stopping her advance.

Michael stepped closer, his smile feral. "You were always feisty, Erin. Maybe I should have taken you first instead of your sister. But she was a good fuck, screaming for me to ram into her. Too bad it ended like it did."

Enraged, Erin swung out, but Leo pulled her back. She struggled, fighting his iron-like grip to the sound of Michael's laughter. "I'll get you, you bastard! You'll pay for killing my family!" She managed to raise her machete.

Michael's laughter subsided, and he backed away. Even Eva seemed less amused.

"Not now, *mia amore*," Leo whispered against her temple. "This isn't the time. He'd kill you in seconds. Wait."

Erin heard the words, but they didn't completely sink in. The bastard mocked her with each breath he took, and she wanted desperately to exact revenge for the memories that haunted her. Images of her mother with her throat shredded. Her father lying in a pool of blood, his face drained of color, skin white as paste. Then Karen—poor Karen. The devil had screwed her before her parents' eyes as their life drained from them. And Erin, conscious and aware the entire night, yet immobilized by some sort of vampiric magic. Michael had been cruel in saving her for last. She remembered his words as he rose from Karen's limp, lifeless body, his lips dripping red. "Sweet little girl, virginal blood is a delicacy to be savored. And as I drink from you, I'm going to send you into ecstasy and you'll give that precious hymen to me." His laughter echoed in her mind even now.

But Leo's gentle hold reassured her. Perhaps he was right. Any attempt on her part right now might end her hunt with her own death.

"I'll bide my time," she said in a low voice, venom tracing each syllable.

When Michael laughed again, she fought from lashing out. Within Leo's arms, she felt protected, but at the same time he gave her a feeling of equality. He stood with her toe to toe against her foe, silently promising to fight by her side.

At that moment, she realized this man—this vampire—was meant to be in her life. He had said she was his life-mate. It must be true.

And she liked the idea.

Could a slayer and a vampire truly overcome their differences and fall in love?

At that moment, she hoped so.

* * * * *

Leo glared at Michael and Eva as they faded into the night. The confrontation wasn't over—they would soon meet again. If Leo knew his brother, Michael wouldn't rest until Erin was dead.

What exactly was her reason for hating Michael? No doubt it was horrific. Perhaps Erin would open up to him and share her story.

"Would you like to go inside?" she asked, bringing his gaze back to her as they finished dressing. Lord, she was beautiful, and her auburn hair was wild and unruly, just like her spirit. He loved that untamable quality about her.

He knew she liked to take control, but in her deepest self, longed to relinquish that control in order to be loved. How fortunate Leo was to find a life-mate that longed for the exact type of sexual play he preferred. Just the remembrance of her toying with her clit on his command made his body harden once again.

"Do you wish for me to go in?" He wanted to test her desires. As they proceeded in this relationship, her ultimate sacrifice would be required.

"Yes," she whispered, stepping closer. The sexual heat poured off her body and called to his. She placed her hand on his chest. "I want you to make love to me."

His eyebrows shot up. Before, she'd wanted to "be fucked". Now she wanted to "make love". Had her feelings for him changed in a few passing moments?

"*Mia amore,* you are my life-mate. I wish to love you for all eternity. Can you understand the commitment and price for me to love you?"

She stood in silence then rested her head against his chest. "I understand."

He tilted her chin so he could look into her eyes. Within the blue depths, he saw a new light. Perhaps it was possible for a slayer to love a vampire.

"Which floor do you live on?" he asked, scooping her into his arms and walking to the edge of the roof.

"Third floor, fourth window from the left."

He transformed into a mist, cradling her in his ghostly form. She nestled and he flew through the air to her window. With a brush of his cloudy hand it opened, and they drifted inside.

In her apartment, he transformed back into his natural form. She seemed unaffected by his transformations. "No surprising you, is there?"

Lying down upon the white comforter of her bed, she moaned, "I've seen more than you can know."

While working on stripping away her clothes again, he let his hands ease over her skin, massaging her muscles in small circles, relaxing her into his touch. "Want to tell me what happened?"

The muscles in her legs tensed, every inch beneath his fingers bunched. He had been reluctant to ask the question, but he needed to know the answer. It might help them in the coming battle with Michael. He caressed her body, starting with the arch of her foot and slowly working his way up.

"He killed my family right in front of me. The memories of that horrible night will live with me forever." She continued to tell him of the way Michael romanced her sister to get inside their home, only to make a feast of them. She also told him of the man who saved her and later trained her to become a slayer.

Leo knew Casey all too well—a menace to the vampire community wherever he chose to hunt. He was ignorant in picking his prey, killing vampires who didn't deserve to meet such cruel deaths. In doing so he had marked himself and was eventually hunted down and killed. Leo remembered that night on the bayou, having been the leader of a band of vampires who had hunted the hunter. That Erin admitted to having feelings for Casey was indeed an unfortunate development.

"Erin, *mia dolce*, I hate to tell you this, but about Casey—"

"I know he's dead. I heard about it through the hunting community."

"He was killing innocents."

She sat up and slid away from him. "No, he wasn't." She cocked her head. "But how would you know?"

He sighed and sat on the bed, his back to her, another trial for them to confront. Those from opposite worlds shouldn't fall in love. "Because I led the search for him. One of my duties is to protect the vampire community from slayers."

She gasped then whispered, "Like me."

He turned and nodded.

"So what will you do to me?"

"For killing Ti, I'm supposed to destroy you." He paused. "Instead, I propose you come with us, join us, help us protect others from those who endanger our existence." He looked into her eyes, reading her confusion. "You know there are demons among us. As I told you, there are the good and the bad. You can help us hunt down the demons that threaten everything and everyone that crosses their paths."

Silence enveloped the room as she considered his suggestion. He knew it wouldn't be easy for her to digest after spending much of her life hunting all vampires.

She sighed then lifted a hand toward him. "I can't explain the connection between us, Leo. I've never felt such emotions before, but I don't want it to end. If you think I can help by hunting the evil of your kind while also giving us the chance to love forever, then it is all right by me."

He took her hand. "I promise—eternal love is what I'll give you. There's no other for me."

She tugged on his arm, urging him to cover her body as she lay back on the bed. Lying upon her felt more intoxicating than any wine. Clad only in panties and a bra, she had on way too many clothes, but he had no time to pull away. She opened her legs and clamped her thighs about his hips, inviting his cock to seek the warm moisture of her core. His chest rubbed against her silk-covered breasts, but nothing could hide the hard points. They seared into him like hot tips of desire, pulsating heat with each touch.

Her body fit perfectly to his, her softness meshed with his hard muscles, yet he could feel strength in her toned body. She was fit for her job, and just staying alive all these years proved she had the talent and the power to defeat any obstacle that would cross her path. He couldn't love her any more than he did right now. She was the woman who could fight by his side, and he would have no worries about her abilities.

Running his hands over her curves, from her hips up to her waist and to her chest, he wanted more than anything to worship her. He brushed a stray strand of auburn hair from her face and looked deep into her eyes, bright with newfound love. No, she may not have actually uttered that word, but he saw it in her eyes.

He covered her lips in a gentle kiss, wanting to show her his deepest devotion. Tenderness was called for. Earlier they had rutted to ease their carnal desires, but now he needed to show her he could be a considerate lover, gentle and caring.

Her soft and inviting lips opened to receive his mouth. He deepened the kiss, plunging his tongue into her sweet mouth, tasting her unique flavor and relishing it. She had a taste that could drug any man, but this was only for him. No other would ever know the intimacies of this woman.

Erin was his.

He broke the kiss and gazed down into her flushed face. Passion suited her—she never looked more beautiful than with the pink blush of desire.

"Erin, are you sure you want to…become a vampire?"

The love that shone in her eyes made him lose his breath. "Bite me, Leo. I want to be yours forever."

Heat surged through his veins as his desire surfaced. She had given permission for him to drink from her—the ultimate sexual high for a vampire and his mate.

His cock was hard and pulsing with eagerness to enter her. He pulled aside the crotch of her panties and slipped into her wet folds. He gasped at the heat surrounding him. It felt as though liquid fire engulfed him in a velvet sheath made just for him. As he began to move within her, she moaned, making it difficult to hold back any control. When she screamed out in a quick orgasm, it sent all reason flying into the night.

At her neck, he bit through the soft flesh to her vein, drinking the precious fluid coursing through her body. By God, it tasted like the sweetest honey!

Erin was his life-mate for all eternity…

But first, they had to destroy her greatest enemy—his brother.

* * * * *

Erin had never felt such pain as when Leo started the process of her transformation. She knew she must come close to death then be returned, with him giving the fluid she needed to complete the change.

He sliced his wrist with a fang protruding from his mouth and offered the blood to her. She was hungry, and as she drank, the sensations that racked her body became unbearable.

At some point, Erin passed out from the pain.

When she awoke, she was unsure of her surroundings and how much time had passed. The pain, however, had ebbed to a dull ache—and an unbelievable hunger.

"Erin, *mia amore*, wake up. The night awaits us."

She groaned as she moved, while her stomach growled. "What happened? Where am I?" Darkness surrounded them, but she could make out his silhouette next to her.

"After we exchanged blood last night, I brought you here to my resting place to wait out the daylight."

She sat straight up in shock. "I slept the entire day without knowing it?"

He chuckled as he brought her hand to his lips. "*Mia dolce*, that is normal for a fledgling. Right now you need to feed, and then we shall prepare for the battle tonight."

"Feed? Battle?" Damn, she had been knocked out a long time!

His fangs grew before her eyes as he nibbled the pulse point in her wrist. The tips grazed across her skin, sending tiny shivers along her nerves. "Feed from me then we'll make plans to meet Michael."

She watched in wonder as he took his own wrist and ripped open the skin. Dark blood flowed forth. Bringing his wrist to her lips, she realized the extent of her hunger. She thought drinking blood would repulse her, but his blood tasted exquisite. She glanced into his face, where she saw ecstasy etched in each line.

"Drinking the blood of one's mate is very sexual, *mia amore*."

She couldn't deny that. Her own body seemed to respond to the rich fluid she drank from him. Hot liquid tricked down her throat as her pussy flooded with a different kind of moist heat. Her clit ached for his touch, and she wanted to shatter in his arms as she took in her nourishment.

It was then she realized she lay naked, her skin burning against him as he ripped away his wrist from her lips and closed down upon them in a possessive kiss. His body engulfed hers as he quickly entered her core. White-hot cream surrounded his cock and the satiny walls milked him into her farther.

Within a few brisk and urgent thrusts, he sank his fangs into her neck and came. Shots of searing hot semen flowed into her as he drank from her vein. She convulsed around him and joined him in the towering inferno of passion.

They spoke no words during this quick coupling—a taking to answer the needs of each. She wanted to have him drink from her over and over. Paired with the steely length of his penis within her channel, she prepared to orgasm once again.

"Shhh...*mia dolce*. We have the rest of eternity to mate with each other."

"Can't we just stay here and fuck all night long? I just need you inside me, Leo." She couldn't believe she was saying this, the hunter who had long denied her womanly needs. Now she just wanted Leo to use her body for his pleasure...and hers.

He sighed as his cock slipped from her sheath. "As much as that sounds like a dream, we have something to do first." He backed away and reached for a nearby shirt. "Michael will come again tonight. He will know you are now one of us. You're not safe until he's dead."

Chapter Twelve

Michael! Suddenly serious, she sat up in bed. "When will he come? And where?"

"Knowing my brother, he is already close. He'll be bringing a few friends for this final battle. He knows it is either he or I who will come out of it alive."

"How many do you think he'll bring?" she asked, scurrying around the small, dark room for her clothes. Her feet touched carpet. "Can we have a light on, please?"

"Oh yes, sorry." He flicked on a small lamp that gave off dim illumination.

"Where are we?" she asked, stopping to look about the stony walls.

"My tomb."

I should have guessed, she thought.

"Your sight will improve as you feed more. Soon, the night will be as clear as day. You'll pick up scents on the wind and increase in strength with time." He dressed and stepped to the door. It opened without any visible help, and he peered out.

"Will we get any help in this battle?" she asked, slipping on her overcoat and securing her machete in the inner pocket. She was ready.

Leo turned to her and took her by the shoulders. "We will do this as a team. Together with my friends, we will destroy the creature that murdered your family."

He caressed her with a new mental connection, and she felt the tension ebb from her muscles. They were about to complete her life-long quest together—she and her mate.

"Leo, we're ready," a voice called from outside.

Leo planted a kiss on Erin's forehead. "Are you ready?"

She nodded. "This is the night that Michael pays."

The door to the tomb opened wider with a magical hand. Erin saw four males, one female and a lone wolf waiting outside.

"Leo, we're all here to help," said a handsome Italian man Leo introduced as Alonso. He kept a hand upon the pretty woman beside him, his mate, Jolie.

But the big blond male looked more menacing. Impeccably dressed, he carried a cane with a silver tip on the end. The large gray wolf leaned against his leg. "Michael dares to come into our town to hunt? I warned him not to ever come into my hunting grounds." He stepped forward and bowed to Erin. "Forgive me. My name is Lucius."

Leo went on to introduce Tala, Lucius' wolfen mate, and the two other male vampires, Raife and Vincente.

The latter two were both dressed like pirates, complete with rapiers fastened to their hips. At Erin's questioning look, Raife explained in a clipped British accent, "We were going to do some fencing practice at Pirate's Alley when we heard the word about Michael threatening Leo's mate."

Vincente, a Spaniard with olive skin and long, black hair tied into a queue, offered his hand and swept down in an elegant bow. "You're a beauty, *señorita*. It's my pleasure to help destroy the enemies of my friends and their mates."

"All right, enough is enough, Vince. Don't try and romance my mate away from me on her first night."

Vince laughed as he backed away to stand next to Raife. "Can't blame a horny vampire for trying, *el amigo*."

"Well, isn't this a heartwarming scene," a voice said from behind them.

Erin inhaled the evil vampire's scent, along with the scents of two other males and the woman, Eva.

Tala growled and stood by Lucius. He patted her silvery coat in a calming gesture.

"You all came together just to face me?" Michael laughed as he and his companions began circling.

Each male radiated danger, and Erin grasped a stake from her inner pocket but kept it hidden. At the first chance, she'd immobilize that bastard Michael.

But how could she possibly get close enough?

"Michael, I warned you never to come to my hunting grounds." Lucius stepped forward. He appeared calm in this crowd of masculine vampiric power.

"Lucius, you Viking raider. I see you got yourself a wolf-bitch. Why the hell would you care about where I hunted?"

Growling low, Tala stepped forward, but Lucius still talked in a cool manner. "I would be careful how you talk about my mate. She has a certain dislike for bastards born to whores."

Erin gasped and turned to Leo.

"Michael is illegitimate. My father had a mistress," Leo whispered into her thoughts.

Michael glared at Tala and Lucius then backed off a step to proceed toward Erin and Leo.

"Raife, darling, long time, no see, my love." Eva broke from the other vampires and edged up to Raife. "I think it has been…what? Two centuries since I felt you between my thighs? I could use your special brand of loving, sweetheart." She grasped his crotch and rubbed his cock through the material. "You always had an impressive sword to impale me with, darling," she added in a low husky voice.

Raife grabbed her wrist and ripped her hand from his groin. "I wouldn't want to fuck you if you were the last female on earth."

Her eyes slid between Riafe and Vince then she smiled coyly. "Perhaps you two would like to have a threesome. Both of you could fuck me at once. I'd give you the best head you ever had this side of eternity. I—"

"Enough!" Vince commanded, unsheathing his sword and pointing it under her chin. "We're not interested, so back off."

"Eva," Michael interrupted. "Get back with the others…now."

"But—"

"I said now!" Michael raised his arm, and the female vampire flew backward with an invisible push.

Erin had noted Michael's interest in Eva's attempts at seduction. He got visibly excited at her suggestions, and when Raife and Vince declined, he seemed disappointed. Could a similar tactic by her turn him on? At least so she could get close enough to stake him? Worth a shot!

"You shouldn't have told her I was illegitimate, brother. That wasn't very nice."

He had heard their thoughts? But of course—they shared the ultimate blood bond—same parents. Or in their case, a shared parent. Erin decided she couldn't let Leo in on her plan to get close to Michael.

"I warned you about her, Leo. She wasn't meant to become one of us. Think of all the vampires she's killed. Now you lie with a slayer. You, my brother, are the enemy." Michael paused in front of them, unaffected by the other vampires.

Cocky bastard.

"I'm not the enemy, Michael. You are. You kill for the joy of it, the physical rush of a most deplorable kind. You're the one who needs to be destroyed!"

"After this night, brother, you'll never have to worry about seeing me again. I'll leave you out to face the sun while I take your little cunt and fuck her in every orifice. It'll be for me to screw her virginal anus into the next century, and all the while, the one who made her a vampire will be long forgotten."

Leo's anger became palpable, and the muscles in his jaw twitched in irritation. Erin found her chance. She just prayed Leo would forgive her.

* * * * *

Leo wanted to throttle his half-brother. The bastard had existed way too long. And threatening Erin went beyond the limits. Just the slightest thought of her with anyone else but him became unbearable.

Just as he prepared to slash that smile from Michael's face, Erin purred next to him, "Oh wow—fuck me in every way imaginable? I have to say, that is tempting."

"What the fuck are you doing?" he mentally asked, but she refused to answer.

Michael laughed as he wrapped an arm about her waist. "All it took was a taste of blood to see the glorious darkness." He leaned toward her ear. "You fought so long against us, and now you are one of us. You shall replace Eva as my mate, Erin, and we shall rule the vampires to hunt and kill. Imagine all the feasts we shall have. Then I will fill you to the hilt. Oh yes, I can see it now, fucking your ass as you drink from your latest victim."

When Michael licked her cheek in a gross gesture, it proved too much for Leonardo. Everything seemed to snap at once.

Erin whipped out her stake and plunged it into Michael's chest. His scream filled the night and he clutched her hair, drawing her with him as he backed away in pain. Blood gushed from around the wound, spraying red upon Erin and the surrounding tombs.

The other enemy vampires advanced, and Lucius, Tala, Alonso and Jolie took action. The sounds of ripping flesh and vicious howls rent the air.

Eva screeched and flew toward Michael, still holding Erin by the hair. Raife and Vincente stopped her. Swords cut through the air and her skin, slicing her throat, clogging her voice with bubbling blood. She grasped the pumping wound and hissed before transforming into a mist and disappearing into the night. Raife and Vincente nodded at each other before also shifting into clouds of mist.

Leo advanced upon the struggling Michael, but cautiously—his hold on Erin's hair dragged her with him. Michael eventually staggered and fell, losing his grip on Erin.

Behind them, the sounds of the fight faded into silence as their friends defeated Michael's henchmen.

"Time to die," Leo promised calmly.

Blood seeped from Michael's mouth. "You don't have the stomach to kill me, brother. I am your own blood. You can't do it."

Leo looked solemn as he watched Michael beg for his existence. But he couldn't let him live. He'd continually be a danger to all.

"It's not Leo's place to kill you, vampire!" Erin spat as she pulled the machete from her trench coat. "That pleasure is all mine. It's past time you went to hell."

In a split second, she lifted the weapon and severed Michael's head from his struggling body.

Leo exhaled, unaware he had been holding his breath.

Erin stood over the body, breathing deeply as she calmed her own nerves. Leo took her into his arms. She dropped the machete and it landed with a thump next to the corpse.

"It's over. It's over," she repeated as she held Leo tight.

"Leo, Eva got away. We took off after her but lost her," Raife said behind them.

Leo turned with Erin still in his arms. "She'll have to recover before she appears again."

He gazed at Lucius and Alonso, both stroking their mates. Tala, still in wolf form, nuzzled against Lucius as he whispered to her in soft tones. Alonso held a shaking Jolie, apparently surprised by her newfound strength and abilities.

"Well, Leo," Raife said, "I think you have a night of hunting with your mate ahead of you. Vince and I, however, have plans at Pirate's Alley. After we clean up this mess, we're heading out."

Leo nodded and led Erin into the cemetery, now eerily quiet compared to only moments ago. He soon felt the others depart, leaving them alone.

He looked over his shoulder. The several vampire corpses and their detached parts had been gathered into a pile. With a wave of Leo's hand, the mound burst into flames. Ordinarily, he would have let the sun incinerate the remains, but being early in the night, he felt it better to take care no one tripped over a body. The sun would burn away anything left behind.

"How about we get cleaned up before we find our meals?" he said as they stopped walking. The moon shone brightly, and the flickering flames behind them lit the night. Apart from the crackles of fire, he heard only the heartbeats of small animals scurrying among the tombs.

"Just promise me something first," she said, tilting her head toward his.

"What?"

"That I never turn into a beast like Michael."

He kissed her forehead and held her by the back of the head, relishing her silky hair beneath his fingers. "That could never happen. Michael was disturbed when he was mortal. Turning vampire only amplified his problems."

"And one more thing."

"Whatever you wish."

"Love me forever. Don't ever stop."

"I'll always love you, Erin. That is something I can't help even if I tried."

She wrapped her arms about his neck and whispered against his lips, "I love you, Leo."

"I love you too, *mia* slayer *dolce*. For all eternity."

Chapter Thirteen

Raife

She murmured in his mind, *"Come to me, my love."*

Powerless to resist her spell, he trotted through the streets of the French Quarter. A force beyond his control led him onward, searching for the one she called.

He was her familiar, her loyal companion and her advisor. Tonight, Yvette had once again taken destiny into her own hands and cast the spell for him, Claude, to bring back the man destined to be her paramour.

Yvette had cast this same spell before through the years, but after a strange dream the previous night, she awoke, sure that tonight she would find her one true love.

Through the bond she would find with this destined love, Yvette could increase the strength of her magic more than ever before. There was always a price to be paid to the Divine for the magic she used, and in her case, power came from sexual gratification. Pleasure from orgasm combined with the power of love could never be surpassed.

Unfortunately, at thirty-four, his mistress was losing hope of ever finding that one true love.

At times, Claude felt sorry for her when the loneliness ate at her soul, and he was her only comfort. But a cat had limited abilities. They could discuss things with their mental connection, but he couldn't give her the love of a soul mate.

He was among the Blessed creatures put on Earth to guide and protect those gifted by the Divine. Many of his relatives were guardians for their human counterparts. Claude had been with his mistress in her current life since he found her when she was seventeen. Like some of the other sacred pets charged to guard the priestesses, Claude was immortal. As one of the Blessed humans, Yvette's soul was also immortal. Her body was human, but her spirit regenerated and returned to Earth in different forms. Her magical talents took a toll on her mortal life.

His mistress had grown up gifted with special talents that set her apart from her peers. In this incarnation, she had gone through life in New Orleans drawn to the rituals and beliefs of the many residents of the past. She felt the most comfortable while practicing the magical arts.

Onward he padded, toward strange cheering punctuated by the sound of steel against steel. What could be making such a ruckus? As he came into the area known as Pirate's Alley—located between Chartres and Royal streets and separating the Spanish Cabildo from St. Louis Cathedral—Claude remembered hearing tales of ghostly pirates reliving their bygone days. It was said that echoes of slave auctions could be heard in the dead of night in the haunted alley.

Claude shivered. Vampires, werewolves, ghosts…all were possible, and many humans believed they were mere bedtime stories. If a cat can be a witch's familiar, a soul guide, *anything* was possible. And all of the supernatural elements seemed to converge in New Orleans.

Mist inched along the moist ground, carrying the ghostly voices of the long dead. Ghosts. Spirits. Claude recognized what they were—being privy to conversations between his mistress and her clients who wished to contact the deceased. But this was his first personal experience with ghosts.

He took a deep breath, all the while hearing Yvette whisper in his mind, *"Come to me and sample the sweets of love. I call to you, mon chere."*

Claude knew the message would be heard by the one man—the only one—who could answer Yvette's prayer.

There before him, the souls of the dead were very much stirring. Cheering and yelling at the two clashing swords that filled the air. Claude sat and watched the men—no, not men. Something else, something…

Claude sniffed the air and caught their scent. He groaned inwardly, if cats could be allowed such a noise. Vampire. The scent was unmistakable. It was close to the cat-shifter scent, but more potent with...evil. Although these two duelists didn't seem evil, laughing and fighting before the jovial pirate ghost crowd.

One of the vampires looked up, and his masculine beauty—blue eyes, dusty blond hair and a muscular physique—struck Claude. A perfect mate for his mistress.

The pair stopped their duel, and the one who heard Yvette turned to Claude. Realization filled the vampire's eyes and Claude approached him.

* * * * *

Rapists, murderers and criminals…they had made up the base of the original population in New Orleans. Even after death, they still haunted the city's bars and hotels. But only in Pirate's Alley did they gather to relive their glories.

Among voices rising in excitement, steel clashed against steel. Raife and Vincente practiced here in order to remain close to their departed friends. Dueling reminded them of their glory days of sailing the seas and fighting for their countries. In life, Raife and Vincente had been enemies. Now, centuries later, they were comrades.

As they fenced for the crowd, a voice came loud and clear through the cheers—a feminine voice singing.

Raife held up his hand and stopped Vincente's advance. The ghostly audience moaned and groaned in disappointment, for the fight had been going so well.

"You hear that?" Raife asked his friend.

Vince laughed. "I don't hear anything but our *amigos* screaming for me to finish you off."

Raife heard the voice calling to him more clearly…

"Come to me and sample the sweets of love. I call to you, mon chere."

He looked around, searching for the source of the voice, so sweet in tone.

Then, trotting amid the pirates' spirits, a black cat appeared on the field of battle and rubbed against Raife's legs.

He picked up the cat and looked intently at it. Then he heard her again.

"I call to you. Come to me…"

"What is it, *amigo*?" Vince asked.

The cat mewed, and Raife knew it had answered the question. This cat was a familiar, which would mean—a witch sent him.

A witch called to him…and he felt powerless to resist…

After placing the cat on the ground, he unfastened his scabbard from his hips and handed it, along with his sword, to Vincente. "Hold on to these for me." Turning back to the cat, now gazing up at him with piercing green eyes, Raife instructed, "Take me to her."

"*Amigo*, are you sure this is such a good idea?"

The cat took a few steps then glanced back at Raife, waiting for him to follow. "It's obvious I'm expected. I don't feel any immediate danger, but if that changes, I'll call you."

Vincente nodded.

Raife stepped after the cat, which trotted ahead into the deserted street.

"Yes, mon amour, come to me. Love me," her voice whispered as he followed the feline familiar. It seemed the voice came from the cat or was directed through it.

Images of supple flesh caressed his mind. Why did she call to him alone? Why hadn't Vince heard her? What sort of magic beckoned?

This night was full of surprises. Only hours ago he had fought against some of the more unsavory creatures, Eva among them. Seeing her again had brought a wave of pain and emptiness. Raife had loved her so long ago, and the ache of her cruel actions had left scars upon his heart. She was evil, a *demoni,* and she had gotten away.

He cursed himself for letting her escape the end of his sword. Running her through, however, would have been too good for the likes of her. She had spent centuries turning unknowing humans into vampires and seducing them into her service. Raife was one of her victims.

He hated the sight of her—the mere thought of her made him sick. But still, she retained the flawless beauty of a goddess. Too bad she possessed a heart of ice and a cruel streak that ran deeper than the Atlantic Ocean.

Since the days when Eva had ripped open Raife's soul, women in his life came few and far between. They were delights in the feed, or satiation to his sexual urges, but he preferred female vampires to the delicate life of a human woman. Aware that many humans couldn't withstand the harsh mating of an immortal, he made sure he never took any chances.

The cat continued to trot along the street. A few humans and vampires stalked the shadows—some predators, some victims. The vampires that recognized Raife slid back out of sight. They hunted, and when bloodlust hit, some had a hard time keeping the beast at bay. Raife had no problem controlling his inner demon, but newer vampires struggled to keep the balance of good and evil.

In the beginning, Raife had been much like those fledgling creatures. If not for Leonardo, he probably would have greeted the dawn long ago. Leo had picked him up while feasting upon whores in England, at the time of Elizabeth I. Earlier that same evening, his inability to age had been met with accusations of demon's magic. Leo knew it was time to move on.

Raife and Leo began their friendship and traveled the world to sate their hungers. When they eventually arrived in New Orleans, they met Vincente, turned during the same time period as Raife. The vampires became friends despite their different cultures and upbringing. Long ago, as a loyal Englishman, Raife would have hated Vince and his Spanish blood, but they shared a similar love—the sea.

They spent hours reminiscing about the days of old, fighting for king and country upon the seas. Nothing could invigorate a man more than the feel of the wind and salt spray against the skin. They understood that passion and became fast friends. Nights of fencing in Pirate's Alley were only one of the things they did to recapture the past.

The cat disappeared into a building ahead. Raife mused at the sign high above the street. "Bell, Book and Candle," he said and chuckled. Appropriate. Like Jimmy Stewart's character in the movie of the same name, he was being drawn into the witch's lair by magic.

He stepped to the doorway and peered inside. In the darkness, he saw the figure of a woman silhouetted against the soft glow of candlelight. She leaned over, picked up the cat and purred to it.

"Come in, *mon chere*," she said in a melodious voice that vibrated through Raife's entire being.

He stood transfixed by the heavenly sight of her stoking her pet. Long-denied sensations surged to life.

"Do you fear me?" she asked as she placed her familiar on a nearby counter.

"No," he replied, crossing the threshold of her store.

Various items pertaining to magic and witchcraft lined the walls. Spell books crammed shelves, while candles and crystal beads, Tarot decks and other paraphernalia lay everywhere. Rich green velvets covered several tables, all arranged with attractive displays of crystal balls, and stones like quartz, tiger's eye and amethyst. Incense filled the air with the scent of lavender. It wrapped about Raife's body with wispy fingers, comforting and inviting. He breathed deeply, letting the magical essence soothe his apprehensions.

He smelled her scent, purely woman, utterly female. Even the fragrance of her excitement drifted through the air, calling to him to taste the sweet honey between her legs.

"Why did you call to me?" he whispered, unable to deny his arousal at her closeness.

"Because only *you* can fulfill my needs."

"And those would be?" He took another step closer. Her features lay in darkness, but his ethereal eyes made out her classic beauty—skin like creamy cappuccino, and eyes dark as obsidian gemstones, black and mysterious but bright and sparkling.

"I need love, *mon chere*. Only the one who could fulfill my need heard my call."

"I heard you," he replied in a husky voice.

"I know." She moved toward him, closing the distance between them, and he saw her more clearly. She was of an exotic heritage, probably Creole, and extremely beautiful. Her skin was smooth, and her lips were full and red, almost silently begging him to kiss them.

"And now that I am here, what do you intend to do?"

She touched him above the small V of his shirt. Her fingertips burned against his exposed skin, not at all unpleasant. "I want you to make love to me."

This was more than any man could take. Hell, he was a vampire. Didn't she understand he could kill her? A vampire could easily rip apart a human lover.

"I'm not an ordinary man, love. I'm…beyond human."

She pressed her body against his. Her heat called out to him. "I know what you are. It doesn't matter. You are meant to be mine."

He raised his hands and tightly held her upper arms. "A witch is still mortal. You tempt me too far. Beware, this isn't something to take lightly."

Leaning closer, she touched the sensitive base of his neck with her tongue. She was seducing him into her world. He had followed her familiar into her lair, and now he was at the mercy of a witch.

Her warm, moist tongue danced over his skin. She unbuttoned his shirt, allowing herself access to his chest. As she licked his skin, Raife moaned. When she teased one of his nipples, he held her head to him, urging her to continue. She gently bit the erect nipple, and he about lost control. How much could a man take when a beautiful seductress tantalized his senses with such expertise?

Grasping her head between his hands, her silky, long tresses caressing his fingers, he gazed at her face. Such a creature couldn't be real. Was she a vision made to tempt him for some other reason?

Her tongue flicked out and ran over her upper lip, her eyelids closed with heavy desire. Her breath became labored and quick, while excitement edged every feature of her face. Raife heard the pounding of her heart and the flow of rich, hot blood coursing through her veins. Such a temptation.

One he wouldn't resist tonight.

He closed his lips over hers and surrendered himself to the power of this enchanting woman.

Chapter Fourteen

Yvette couldn't control her body's yearnings. When this man had approached her Wiccan supply shop, she had felt his true nature.

Vampire…

So be it. A vampire was more than she could have hoped for. His immortality would give her exactly what she needed.

She had been a witch all her life and in all her past lives. Magic was her close companion, wrapping her in its protective embrace. After she called upon her powers, however, they needed to be replenished. Sexual desire and passion were driving forces of humanity, and for her they were her means to repay the goddesses for their gift of magic. Orgasm usually met the requirements of repayment, but as she aged, she needed more—she needed love, eternal and true. Paired with the strength of love, the act held incredible power and energized her Wiccan charm.

Last night she dreamed of a man, strong and virile. He lurked nearby, just within reach. His dream form touched her and spasms racked her into wakefulness. She climaxed at the merest touch of his dream-state hand.

Summoning the goddesses that evening, she chanted a spell, calling to her destined lover to come to her. Sending Claude into the city had broadened the call, homing in on the one to answer her prayers.

When he had approached her shop, Yvette immediately realized he was an immortal, a vampire. Her body quickened at his presence as he stood under the soft street light. Her cunt instantly ached for his cock to fill her to the hilt. Images of him beating into her body, setting the scene for a powerful orgasm, flashed through her mind, and her pussy wept in want.

She had invited him into her store, burning to feel his naked flesh against her own. His long blond hair fell about his shoulders in a wild, untamed manner, and his sapphire eyes caressed her with their heated gaze. She was drawn to him beyond her own understanding. The need to feel his skin against her tongue was too tempting.

He fought for control, but she seduced him like an expert, drawing upon her power of sexual allure to ease him into her trap.

It *was* a trap. She wanted to imprison this handsome vampire within her arms, and have him submit to her kisses. He resisted, but the soft press of her body against his apparently became too much, and he let all inhibitions fly and raped her mouth with his own.

With her palms, she mapped the hard planes of muscles along his back and shoulders, and judging from his quick intake of air, it excited him more. His tongue plundered her mouth in hot strokes, drinking her into his senses.

"Witch," he murmured as he nibbled her jaw. She felt his fangs scrape along her skin, and she inhaled sharply at the pleasurable pain.

Sighing, she dropped back her head to allow him better access to her neck. Somehow, the want for him to drink from her grew overwhelming. As much as she planned to take from him all he had to offer—love and sexual gratification—she wanted to give in return.

Where did that desire come from? She was so used to taking from men when she tempted them with her power, but this was different. This was more than she had ever expected. He was to be her soul mate.

His fangs sank into her neck.

Her womb clenched in need to have him while he drank. Chills ran across her nerves and heat soaked into her bones.

She felt on fire, and as his body moved against hers, it became the most erotic moment she had ever experienced. His hands molded her form to his, and her aching breasts pressed firmly against his chest. His mouth worked at her vein, and her breath came in quick pants.

Then her body lost restraint in a powerful climax. She gasped and cried aloud, melted against him and his embrace. Burning flames licked at the vessels pumping hot blood through her, and she rode out the ecstasy brought on by this vampire.

He lifted her into his arms and held her while she clutched her legs around his waist. Even through the fabric of his pants, she felt his bulging erection straining to dive into her. It brushed against her sensitive clit, and she shattered again.

She screamed as he steadied her body to ride his hips. He licked at the wound on her neck. His heated tongue caressing her bruised skin made her whimper.

"Your blood is a delicacy, love." He backed her to the cashier counter, setting her rump on the hard wooden surface. His hands left her body briefly as he unbuttoned his jeans and released his cock.

"Oh, yes," she moaned, grasping his rod—so hard and hot—in her palm. She gently squeezed it.

He groaned as he lifted her skirts and yanked off her panties, soaked with her juices. "I'm going to fuck you, sweet witch. That tight pussy is mine tonight."

"Please," she begged in a whisper while holding onto his broad shoulders.

His engorged head paused at her slick entrance, and she involuntarily bucked toward him. He traced her straining clit with his tip, and she tossed her head from one side to another in abandon.

He dipped a finger through her folds as he teased her clit with his cock. He smacked his lips. "Sweet and tempting. Are you as hot and wet inside?" His husky voice held a hint of laughter.

Then, with a slow push, he slid into her.

Wrapping her arms about his neck, pulling him closer, she rode his cock as he plunged in and out of her slick core. She wrapped her legs about his waist and tried to get him deeper within.

"Oh, by the goddesses!" she called when she climaxed about him, his thrusts more frenzied, more urgent, searching for his own release within her tight core.

When he spilled his seed into her, she clutched him tighter with her arms and legs and screamed. Never had an orgasm felt so magical, so completely…wonderful.

She grasped his head between her hands and ran her fingers through the silky strands of his hair then guided his mouth to hers. She fed upon his essence and reveled in it. His immortal seed rejuvenated her spent powers.

And his skilled loving awakened the passion she thought was only fantasy. Men were mere vessels to be used to serve her purpose. But this time, with this vampire, it was different.

She used her magic to find her true love, never really expecting to find it.

And it scared the hell out of her.

* * * * *

Weakness radiated through her body. Blood. She needed blood, and quickly. Her wounds from tonight's battle had taken a toll, but it would take much more than a slice of her jugular to destroy her.

Raife and his Spaniard companion had chased her, but her transformation into mist had delayed the loss of her strength. Regardless of her form, however, her injury still slowed her down.

Eva spiraled through the streets of New Orleans to escape her former lover and his vengeance. Finally, when she felt his presence dissipate, she felt safe to emerge and hunt. She needed to replenish her strength through the blood of a human. Any human would do.

In a back alley, Eva passed a female emptying trash into a Dumpster. An easy target, innocent and fresh. Eva could smell her youth, her virginity upon the wind. Such a treat was even more powerful for the likes of a depleted vampire.

The girl was dressed conservatively and seemed out of place in the dirty alley. Eva watched as the girl stopped and glanced upward toward the moon. Pale illumination upon her skin made her appear angelic, almost unreal. She slipped a stray strand of pale blonde hair back behind her ear and sighed.

Longing and loneliness filled the air about her, and Eva moved in closer. In her misty form, she crawled along the cobblestones with ghostly ease.

Eva clamped her phantom claws about the girl's ankles.

The girl gasped when she realized she was in danger, but she had no time to panic as Eva enveloped her in a misty grasp. Though drained, Eva lifted her victim into the air and disappeared into the darkness.

The girl whimpered and struggled, but to no avail. Eva laughed as she squeezed her meal tighter. Sailing over the city into the remote swamplands, Eva stole the girl. Tonight, she would feed well.

So much had happened tonight. She had lost her mate. Michael had betrayed her. He had thought to replace her with Erin. Bastard. Men were all assholes. Each and every one never proved to be worth much beyond satisfying carnal lusts. Michael was a wonderful lover but a bad vampire. And now she was alone, except for this tantalizing piece of feminine flesh within her embrace.

Perhaps it was time to make a new companion…

* * * * *

"What's your name?" Raife asked, unable to believe he had just had the most incredible sex of his entire existence with a woman he knew nothing about, not even her name.

"Yvette." She paused as she leaned into him. "And you?" Now seated on the floor of the shop, they relaxed together in the afterglow.

"I'm Raife, milady."

She smiled, and her natural beauty warmed him.

"I don't meet vampires every day, though I've felt their presence many times before."

"We dislike magical folk. Or should I say, they naturally dislike us? Generally, we are used to having spells cast to keep us away."

"Well, I certainly didn't expect a vampire to answer my call."

She looked at him with those dark eyes and he wanted to melt. Never had he felt such attraction for a woman. Could it be he had finally found his life-mate?

"And now? Do you regret that I answered?"

Her fingertips traced his jaw in a tender caress. "Never. You were the one destined to answer."

He grasped her fingers and brought them to his lips. "Maybe my loneliness is finally at an end."

"*Mon chere*, I've waited for you so long, but I wonder how this can ever work. You're a vampire, a creature of darkness, whereas I am a woman of magic, a white witch. Our worlds weren't meant to mix."

"We'll get by somehow."

Just then, he felt a jolt—an ominous sensation ripping through his body.

"What is it?" she asked worriedly.

Evil and deceit slammed into his heart, and he could think of only one reason for such powerful angst.

Eva. The vampire had brought another over to the immortal existence. She had damned another soul. Even after all the centuries, he had that connection to his creator. He could sense her thoughts and her actions through the blood bond created so long ago.

"Damn it," he whispered as he drew Yvette closer.

"What is it?"

"Another has been born. The one that created me…she has made another." He explained his creation by Eva and his history with the vampiress. "And tonight I faced her once again, wounding her, but she escaped. Because of me, she still roams. Now she's found another victim to damn."

"Do you need to go?"

He sighed and pulled her closer to his body. Breathing deeply her fresh scent, he said, "Dawn approaches. By the time I go and find Eva and her fledgling, it would be time for me to seek shelter from the sun."

"Must you leave me soon, then?"

"Soon. 'Tis the life of a vampire." He felt saddened that he must leave Yvette behind to rest. Never would the hours of the day seem so long now that he had found his mate.

* * * * *

Another felt the addition of a new vampire to the world, one who knew all too well of Eva's evil. He too had been seduced by her dark allure, only to be cursed into a life he neither wanted nor enjoyed.

Since his woman had died due to a curse upon the mixing of vampire and werewolf blood, he had roamed the earth, pining for his lost love.

"I saw her, Damon. In a vision, I saw her," Tala said, sitting across from him in her small shack on the bayou. There with her vampire lover, Lucius, she explained how they overcame the ancient curse of their kinds.

He and Telia had not been as lucky as Lucius and Tala.

"You saw her? Was she happy?"

"She ran with the phantom pack. She…she said for you to have hope, Damon. You were destined for another."

Impossible.

He felt Eva then…close. And not alone, as she had made another companion to eventually abandon. Just as she had done to him years ago.

"What is it?" Tala asked at his apparent disturbance.

"Eva. She's here. And she brought over another soul into the existence."

"We saw Eva tonight with Michael. She got away, but Michael wasn't so lucky," remarked Lucius as he slid a hand over Tala's shoulders.

Damon was jealous of the connection between them. Though he was not as old as the ancient Lucius, he was in pain. Sometimes it was worse to lose your love rather than never having loved at all.

"She'll desert the fledgling once the novelty of bringing one over has faded. She always does." He rose from the table. "I'll find Eva and her new companion. Her evil must stop."

"Need us to help?" asked Tala as Damon reached the door.

"No. Eva needs to be destroyed by one she created."

With that he went outside, and in the blink of an eye, his size and shape shifted. Feathers replaced skin, claws replaced fingers. As a great gray owl, he soared above the swamplands in search of his creator.

Chapter Fifteen

Yvette took Raife by the hand and led him upstairs to her apartment above the store. While Claude settled in his little bed, she took her new lover to her bedroom.

Turning to him, she said in a husky voice, "Make love to me, Raife. Touch me. Make me yours."

He saw the heat in her eyes. Her heart pounding within her chest resounded in his ears. The blood coursed beneath her skin, tempting him with each heartbeat.

"Yvette, before the sun rises, I'll have learned each inch of your luscious body."

He stepped before her and she breathed deeply as he lifted away the thin barrier of fabric to reveal her perfect cappuccino-colored skin. Like creamy coffee, she was smooth and flawless.

Her long black hair fell loose about her shoulders, and he marveled at her natural beauty. Her lips were made to be kissed, full and ripe.

"Lick your lips," he commanded.

Her obsidian eyes searched his face as her tongue flicked out over her bottom lip. He suppressed a groan as the slow, deliberate motion brought to mind images of that tongue dancing over his skin.

"Close your eyes too."

"But—"

"Trust me, love." Their earlier coupling had been fast and animalistic. Right now, he needed to savor her delights.

Her pink-tipped nipples perfectly complemented her tanned globes. His mouth watered to taste their berry-like texture.

She inhaled quickly when his thumb brushed the sensitive tip. The sound was innocently sexy and utterly feminine.

He stripped out of his clothes and stood naked before her.

The urge to toss her down upon her bed and ram into her deep heat grew overwhelming. He had to pound down the instinct to mate with her until she begged for mercy. He wanted to make this time an experience to enjoy. He wanted this for her pleasure.

Stepping around to her back, he leaned into her, close but not touching. "Yvette, I want to fuck you slow and easy. I want to give you such pleasure. Can you understand this?"

"Yes," she sighed.

"Do you have any idea how beautiful you are? You can draw a man across the sea for one touch of your lips upon his skin."

His hands encircled her body to cup her breasts in his palms, brushing his thumbs across her nipples. She gasped while leaning back into his body.

"I'd fight the Armada all over again just to feel the heat of your skin against mine."

He nestled his cock between her ass cheeks, and she wiggled back in response.

"No battle would keep me from your side. No enemy would prove too deadly to face just for the touch of your hand in mine."

He breathed in the fresh scent of her hair, and she shivered within his arms.

"Even if I would meet the dawn in the morning, my soul could rest for eternity knowing I've loved you tonight, sweet Yvette."

"Oh, Raife..." Her voice was a soft plea.

He picked her up into his arms and held her like a man deprived of love for several lifetimes. She wrapped her arms about his neck and rested her head against his shoulder.

Settling her upon the large bed covered in soft cotton sheets and a fluffy down comforter, he felt almost as if he had laid her in a cloud.

She whimpered at the loss of his closeness then sighed in contentment when he covered her body with his.

"Keep your eyes closed," he said, tracing a line with his finger along the inside of her arm. "Just feel."

Raife proceeded to map her body with his hands. He kneaded her breasts, studying their texture and weight. Her nipples puckered and swelled as he gently squeezed the perfect mounds. Lightly, he continued his exploration of her body, stopping periodically to taste her skin with his tongue. His lips curled around the pert tips of her nipples and her back arched upward in response. Sweet ripeness and ready to be plucked by the right lover, her body moved to a rhythm of ecstasy he made just for them.

When Raife moved his ministrations down her body, Yvette's breathing increased in speed. He could feel her excitement vibrate through her entire being. As he drew close to her center, he teased her labia with light caresses then backed away.

Her trimmed mound called to him, feminine juices flowing from her core to tempt his invasion. But not yet. He wasn't through with his exploration of her. He doubted he ever would be. An eternity would never be enough for him to taste each alluring inch of this woman.

Down her inner thighs, he trailed his fingertips along her soft skin. She moaned and bucked her hips in frustration.

"Patience, little witch. Patience." He nipped the skin next to her knee.

His fangs extended to full length as his vampire instincts clawed to the surface. The man wanted to savor her delights, while the vampire needed her substance.

Using his hands, he parted her thighs wider as he lay between them. He glared at her ripe center, her pink folds revealing her jeweled clit peeping from its hood. His mouth watered. Creamy honey lined the entrance to paradise, and it was all for him.

With one finger, he traced the slippery crease of her folds, ending his torment upon the straining bud. She grasped the sheets beneath her.

"Your body yearns for me to fill it, doesn't it, sweet witch?"

"Yes," she croaked, barely controlled.

"First, I must taste the nectar you've provided for my pleasure."

He slid a finger into her sheath. She cried out.

"Tell me, love. Do you wish for my cock to touch you here?" he asked as his finger moved inside her.

"Oh, God…yes…yes…"

"And right here?" he teased as his thumb stroked her clit while his fingers rhythmically plunged in and out.

"Yes, Raife, oh please, I need…"

"Need me to fuck your sweet cunny, Yvette?"

"Yes."

"Need me to fulfill your desires for the rest of eternity?"

"Yes."

He pulled his slick fingers from her pussy then traced back along her folds to the rosette opening of her anus. "Need me to become your mate?" He pressed his wet fingers into the opening.

She groaned, "Yes, please. Now."

"Tell me what you want me to do to you. Tell me how to fuck you in a way to make you howl in delight at your orgasm."

"Lick me, then fuck me. Oh, please…"

Before Yvette could catch her breath, Raife's lips encircled her bud. As his fingers stroked her openings, he suckled her clit with a gentle suction.

She climaxed as his tongue beat left to right over her nubbin, and his fingers pressed and teased.

Before his lover could recover from her climax, Raife reluctantly lifted his mouth from her apex and followed his darker side. Into her thigh, he sank his teeth. Rich blood, sweet and intoxicating, rushed from her vein down his throat. She orgasmed again from the sheer ecstasy of the vampiric act.

She drugged him in a way he had never felt before. Her body entranced him. He was under her power—the power of budding love and fiery lust.

He knew he'd never be the same again.

* * * * *

As dawn was about to break, Raife left Yvette sleeping in her bed. His body's need to make love again in the early morning called to him, but the need to seek shelter proved even stronger. How he longed to have her rest by his side. His mate, his life companion.

He couldn't just bring her over to this existence. He needed her to ask, to choose him. It was something Eva had denied him when she created him so long ago. With Yvette believing in her own eternal life, reborn each time her physical body died, it would be highly unlikely she would ever choose to become an immortal vampire.

As he made his way to his tomb in St. Louis Cemetery, he heard a voice from the darkness. Used to the scents of many vampires resting here, he hardly took notice. But this one—this one smelled familiar somehow.

This one bore the evil stench of Eva.

"You felt her, didn't you?"

Raife turned and saw a blond vampire move from the shadows.

"You were made by Eva too," Raife stated. It wasn't a question.

"Yes. She's got to be stopped. I went out looking, but all the scents from the swamp make tracking difficult. I'm not as ancient, so my powers are limited."

"I can help. Tonight at ten o'clock, meet me at the Bell, Book and Candle shop in town. We'll plan the hunt and stop Eva once and for all."

"Why so late?"

"My mate may be able to help us. She's a witch. And, well…" Raife knew once he was with Yvette, the need to have her again would overpower him.

The vampire nodded understanding and turned to disappear into the night. He was a stranger to Raife but not totally unknown. Raife had heard of each new creature Eva brought over. It was always an odd occurrence to meet one of her creations. Each had been subjected to Eva's strange sexual longings. Luckily, that usually didn't take place until some nights after the initial turning. Perhaps, when they found Eva and the new vampire, they could save this one from having to deal with Eva's appetite.

* * * * *

Yvette strolled through the St. Louis Cemetery with Claude padding behind. He was much more interested in the mice scurrying along the overgrown weeds than their conversation. Not that he actually hunted the little rodents. Claude was too civilized for such lowly duties, but he still liked to see them run away in fear.

"All these years alone and finally I find the one to love."

"It was fate," Claude whispered in her mind.

"Yes, but to love a vampire…it is beyond my expectations."

"His immorality will give you even more power when he bonds with you."

"I feel the magic coursing through me. But how long can it last? When will he try to bring me over to his way?"

"Would becoming a vampire really be so bad? We can be together for all eternity. I'd never have to search for your reincarnated soul. I'd never have to wait alone while you are reborn."

Claude was sounding more and more convincing. His own immortal life was difficult.

Yvette stepped up to Marie Laveau's tomb and sighed. The teachings of the goddesses told her that her spiritual life was already immortal. Only by becoming a vampire would her physical being become immortal as well.

"What am I to do, milady?" she whispered to the dead Queen. "I longed to love all my life, and even in my prior lives I never found such contentment and peace as I had with one night in the arms of Raife, a vampire. How can this ever work out?"

A gentle breeze kissed her cheek, and Yvette recognized the magical essence of the soul of Marie Laveau. Calming and serene, an overwhelming sense of hope filled her soul. Yvette knew love was destined for her and Raife, but their physical beings threw up barriers to everlasting happiness.

"The choice will be made for you," a soft voice caressed her ears. "Fear not, when the time comes, the heart will follow the right path."

Yvette was used to cryptic messages sent to her in her dreams, but hardly in her waking hours. As quickly as it came, the breeze died away and the voice vanished with it.

"Mistress, I believe we were just granted an extraordinary audience with a powerful being."

"Yes, Claude."

She turned to walk back to her car when a man leapt from behind one of the tombs, grabbing her. Struggling against his strong grip was of no use. The man held her firmly in his grasp as he pulled her back to his chest. A pointed object stuck in her left side, and when she moved it pinched into her skin. She smelled the stench of old liquor upon his breath as he dragged her out of sight.

"Ah, missy, you're a little piece of pleasure made for ol' Jakie. You come here all alone to ease this ache I be havin'?"

He roughly pulled her closer, and Yvette gagged at the pungent odor from his unclean body.

"No sense in strugglin', missy. We be all alone here now. Tourists won't be through for another hour. That gives us plenty of time to play," he chuckled.

Yvette fought the bile in her throat from spewing forth. Why the hell did she come to this area with just Claude? Just to come and visit Marie's tomb? She could've done it anytime, but this was her monthly visit to the Voodoo Queen. And now, she was about to be raped.

Seemingly out of nowhere, Claude pounced at the burly man holding her and scratched his face. The man screamed. In the confusion he let Yvette go, but not before she felt fire burning her skin.

Her hand grasped her side and pulled out the knife the attacker had brandished. Sticky, warm blood oozed from the wound, and she pressed her palm hard against her side to try to staunch the flow.

Turning to the man, she saw him throw down the cat and curse as he noticed her wound. He snatched the dropped knife and disappeared into the cemetery.

Yvette, suddenly weak and helpless, fell to her knees.

"Mistress, are you okay?" a worried Claude asked as he limped to her side.

"You saved me from him, my friend. I don't know if you can help me now."

"You're losing a lot of blood. I should find your mate."

"In the daylight? What can he do to help? I don't even think I can make it to the car."

"I can't let you just lie here and die."

After all the centuries of birth and rebirth, Yvette had finally found the love she craved. And now it was about to slip away.

Unless she fought.

"I refuse to die, Claude. I won't die. Not now. Not when I've found Raife."

"There are a few hours left to daylight. Perhaps if I look for him…"

"There's no need for that." She closed her eyes and opened her soul.

And she called to him.

* * * * *

Her voice, full of pain and sorrow, whispered in his mind, awakening him.

"Raife, my love. I need you." Her plea reached him through his deep slumber in midday.

She was near but hurt. Rage welled up to the surface as he burst from his protective tomb and searched for her. The sun's rays beat down upon his skin, and even at incredible speed, it took a toll upon his form. Burning flesh filled his nostrils as he risked his eternal life for the woman he loved.

Love. It was hard to believe he had fallen in love so quickly. One look of her eyes had entranced him enough to give up his heart, and he never questioned his instant feelings for her.

And now she was in pain, injured and calling for him. Fresh blood in the cemetery drew him, and within seconds he found her. Landing at her side, he slid her body into the shade of a nearby tomb. At least he'd get some relief from the burning ache coursing through his body.

"Yvette, what happened?" he asked, lifting her blood-covered hand from her side. Warm fluid spilled from her body and she was barely conscious.

Her eyes fluttered open for a brief moment. "I came to give thanks to the great Queen but was attacked."

If her life wasn't slipping away so quickly, he would've gone out after the one who dared to touch her, but she needed him here. "You need a hospital."

She fell unconscious. He sensed her heart's erratic beat. She was dying in his arms.

Gathering her up, he waited for the sun to dip behind some clouds. Then he raced with her to the safety of his tomb, barely aware of the cat behind them. Just before Raife slammed shut the stone door, the feline slipped inside.

His skin was afire, red with blisters rising from the short exposure. He was thankful for the cool, welcoming darkness of his resting place. Laying Yvette's limp body upon his bed, he watched in horror as she struggled to breathe once more. He had no choice. He refused to see her die, not after waiting all these long centuries to find her.

Leaning over her, he whispered, "Love, I can't lose you now. I'd go insane without you."

"No," she gasped, but it was too late.

He sank his fangs into the soft flesh of her neck. Never had anything tasted so delectable. Blood burst over his tongue and warmed him on the inside. As he drank from her, the painful blisters swiftly healed. More and more, he drained her of the little blood she had left. He had to force himself to stop before it was too late. Such a delicious feast, he could drink from her and never get enough.

Raife tore his mouth from her neck. Her breathing became extremely ragged. He raised his wrist to his fangs and bit into it, severing a large vein. His life fluid oozed from the broken vessel as he brought it to her mouth.

"Drink, live for me. Become as I. I swear you'll never want for anything again. None shall ever hurt you, my love. I am your mate, your protector."

Her tongue laved at the flowing blood and she became more ferocious in her hunger. As Yvette's lips sucked at his wrist, taking in the essence she needed, Raife tossed back his head and groaned. Sexual want built within him, and he fumbled to release his engorged cock from the tight containment of his jeans.

She continued to drink his blood and his passion rose. Taking his penis in hand, he pumped it to the rhythm of her suckling.

Then she ran her tongue over his wound and gazed into his face. He glanced down at her as her fangs grew before his eyes. The red taint about her lips only excited him further.

He licked the wound at his wrist and it disappeared in a moment. She panted and writhed as she took hold of his cock. Lowering her mouth over the purple head, she began to work her tongue and mouth about his penis.

With one hand, she teased her fingernails over his sack, and he screamed. It was impossible to hold back the ecstasy, and he sprayed heated semen into her receptive mouth. She took it all into her like a starving woman, licking away every trace of his passion. When she gazed up at his face, Raife saw her hunger—sexual desire and want—mixed with fatigue.

"Yvette, you need to rest now, love. You've been stabbed and transformed into…" How would she react to him turning her into a vampire without her permission?

She eased back into the softness of the bed and her eyes fluttered closed. At least she had been spared most of the pain of the turning. She had been so close to death already, there wasn't much suffering involved.

But when Yvette awoke at sunset, Raife feared there'd be a wildcat in his bed, demanding an explanation. She would've forgotten her wound that had already healed.

And then she'd be hungry.

He stripped off his jeans and slid under the sheets next to her. Curling her body to his, he felt right for the first time in ages. This woman, this witch, was truly powerful. The magic she held over him with a simple glance was enough to bring him to his knees. Never had any woman affected his life to such a degree. And now, she was a vampire. She'd be by his side for all eternity, and he'd never let her go.

He rested his head next to hers on the soft down pillow and sighed. Breathing in her musky scent, combined with the scent of his seed and blood, aroused yet comforted him. Running his knuckles over the gentle curve of her hip down to her thigh, he could never imagine life without her.

She was his forevermore.

Chapter Sixteen

"Wake up, love. Time for you to feed."

Her eyelids felt so heavy, she didn't want to open them. She felt strange, and starving. Her stomach cramped and rolled, and she moaned.

"I know—it feels like you've been at sea for three months and starving the whole time. I can't tell you how many times I felt like that back when I was human."

"How long ago was that?" She really hardly knew this man who stood before her, dressing in jeans, sneakers and a white T-shirt. In one way, he looked like any other man, but there in the doorway of the small enclosure, he also looked very much a vampire. Moonlight filtered in around his figure and Yvette marveled at his perfect physique.

Oh yes, perfect.

"I've been a vampire since Elizabeth ruled England. She was my queen and I was one of her privateers. I sailed the seas in her name."

"Jesus, that is like four hundred years ago." Why did she feel like a truck had run over her?

She reached for her side, suddenly remembering the attack. But instead of finding an open wound or even stitches, she felt only smooth flesh.

Then she became aware of her nakedness. She scooted the sheet about her and shot him a questioning glance. "How is this possible?" In her heart, she thought she knew what happened, and almost hated to hear the answer.

"I couldn't let you die, love."

"He saved you, Mistress," piped in Claude as he jumped onto the bed.

"But I had no choice in this," she reasoned with her pet.

"You know, I could swear I heard that cat talk."

"Claude? He's my pet, my companion and my spirit guide."

"But…I heard him. I mean, I hear your thoughts, along with those of others with whom I've bonded, but the cat?"

"Sir, I am no ordinary cat. I am of royal blood, and I've been blessed by the goddess Bast herself. There are several of us feline spirit guides in existence."

"You know what, cat, you're a cocky little puss, but I like you." Humor touched Raife's voice as he leaned down to stroke the cat's black coat.

"Glad to be appreciated," Claude purred.

"But now I'm…a vampire." Yvette could hardly believe the turn of events. The choice had been made for her, just as the Voodoo Queen predicted.

"I'm sorry, love. I couldn't let you die after finding you." Raife knelt and cupped her face in one of his hands. "You're my mate. I would've gone insane without you."

He leaned in and brushed his lips over hers. All of her doubts and anger fled as this incredible being kissed her with the tenderness of a man in love.

A cramp clinched her stomach, and she moaned into his kiss.

"You're hungry. Feed from me," he whispered against her lips.

Desire coursed through her at the thought of tasting him. She vaguely remembered earlier in the day when she had feasted upon his cock, how it helped her magic recover along with her weakened body.

She also remembered feasting upon his blood and the ecstasy it had awakened within her soul.

Her lips pressed to his skin, and she grew aware of the life fluid flowing beneath. She darted out her tongue, ran it along the vein in his neck, and she relished the salty taste. Her mouth ached and she felt her teeth lengthen into fangs. Saliva filled her mouth in anticipation of the coming meal. Then she opened her mouth and followed her instincts. She sank her teeth into Raife's flesh. Blood exploded across her tongue, tangy and addicting. She swallowed and filled her stomach, his rich blood satisfying her hunger. Still, she wanted more.

He groaned and threaded his fingers through her thick hair, clutching her closer to his body roughly. "Yvette, love," he pleaded in a barely controlled voice.

With lightening speed, her fingers worked at the fly of his jeans. After unzipping the material, she pulled out his hard cock and rejoiced at its magnificent size, the hot steel with a satin skin covering, her ideal.

His hands ripped away the thin sheet separating his body from hers. He disposed of his jeans and entered her tight, wet sheath. She screamed as he filled her core to the hilt, breaking her hold upon his neck.

"No, love. More," he gasped, rapidly pumping in and out of her body.

She kissed his neck where the open wound still bled and licked away the trickling blood. Latching her lips around the puncture, she sucked at the vein. With each thrust, she swallowed the hot salty fluid. Lord, if every meal would be so intensely erotic, she wouldn't mind being a vampire.

"You shall feed only from me, love. No other. You're mine."

"Raife, please, fill me," she begged with her thoughts.

In answer, he released the remains of his control and spilled his seed into her womb. Yvette felt her magic empower and pump through her. The euphoric high of ejaculate within her always made her feel alive, invincible. With Raife as her lover, the effect seemed more intense. She had been drained of magic when the attacker struck, but now she collected her price to the goddesses. She had drunk of Raife earlier in the day and still felt the power from the seed he gave so willingly.

Yvette climaxed with him, squeezing his penis in convulsive clenches, riding the waves of passion they had built together. She was in heaven and totally charged.

Moments ticked by, and Raife slid from her center and lay next to her. Moonlight filtered in through the open doorway, and she could see into the night better than she had ever dreamed.

"Isn't it dangerous to leave the door open that way?" she asked in a dreamy voice.

"Humans hunt the unsuspecting vampires during the day, but they stay away at night, knowing the price for wandering here." He paused and looked at her with confusion in his blue eyes.

"What is it?"

"Your skin, it's glowing."

She giggled. "Oh yes, the magic." She told Raife of her payment to the goddesses for their help and guidance in her magic. "When I have an orgasm, I recharge my powers. But when I take in the semen of a man, it is more powerful than with my orgasm alone."

"I guess that explains why you were calling for a lover last night."

"The seed from the man who is my destiny is the ultimate tribute." She ran a finger across his jaw and added in a low voice, "I've longed for love for so long, I was afraid no one would ever answer the call. I'm happy it was you, my pirate-vampire lover."

She pressed her lips to his in a tender kiss.

"Good grief, is this going to take all night? I've had to listen to you two panting and petting and I need to be fed," Claude complained.

"Can't you go catch a mouse or something?" Raife asked as he stood up and pulled on his jeans.

"Catch a mouse? Are you insane? Need I remind you I am of royal blood?" The cat's tone sounded haughty, even to Yvette. Of course, this was nothing new for Claude.

"We'll go to the shop and get your cat food, okay?"

Claude actually sighed into her thoughts. *"I guess so. Once we get there, you can feed me then return to your mating dance. Right now, I'm starved."*

Raife watched the furry animal pad out of the tomb. "I can't believe I have to reason with that hairball. Royal blood, my ass."

"He really is a noble cat and very devoted. He's been there for me in all my forms." She pushed back the covers and slowly stood on shaky legs.

"Here." Raife tossed her a clean T-shirt and a pair of boxers. "These are clean. I'm sorry, but your clothes were ruined. You can get more clothes at your shop."

She nodded.

"There is something else, though. We...we have something to do tonight."

"Like what?" She pulled the large T-shirt over her head and marveled at how her nipples perked at his heated glare. He intently watched her movements, even when their discussion turned away from sex.

"Eva. I met another one of her past creations last night, but he isn't as ancient as I. He asked for my help in tracking her down."

The T-shirt ended at Yvette's hips and the boxers hung on her. Yet Raife still looked at her with desire.

"I'm not sure I like this idea, Raife."

"She has to be stopped." His voice became husky as he stepped closer. "You really do know how to get me all hot and bothered. Just seeing you in my clothes...I can't get enough of you."

He wrapped his arms about her waist. Yvette shivered as he leaned into her, his warm breath tickling her ear.

"I want to fuck you again."

"Already? You just had me."

"Feels like days since I was inside you, love."

"Hey, you two, feed me first, then do your kissy-face stuff!"

"That cat is starting to get on my nerves," Raife said.

They both laughed as they walked out of the tomb.

A chill ran down Yvette's spine as she took in the cemetery. She had slept in a tomb. She had been turned into a vampire. She was a vampire's lover. She had died to become an immortal to be with him. It was a bit much to comprehend. How could she accept everything that had happened in so short a time?

"You'll get through everything with me by your side," Raife whispered into her mind. *"Always know I'll be here for you for the rest of eternity."* He picked her up and cradled her in his arms.

In a flash of ethereal speed, they traveled through the dark New Orleans streets to the Bell, Book and Candle.

* * * * *

Once at the shop, Yvette went to her bedroom above the storefront. Slipping into a pair of jeans and a black turtleneck sweater, she listened to Raife recount more of his history with the twisted Eva.

"She left me alone while I was still a fledgling, hungry and completely unprepared. I learned how to survive, of course. But often I wished to meet the sun, especially when my hunger grew so strong and controlling the blood frenzy became difficult."

She stepped into a pair of dark brown boots and proceeded to lace them. What made him think turning her would be any better? Would she become insane with the need to feed?

"Never worry, love. I'll take care of your needs. The thought of you drinking from another…I couldn't bear it. I shall feed then you will drink from me."

"I like that idea, Raife. I'm not sure I could do it otherwise."

A foreign scent drifted through the air. She could actually smell another vampire—or rather, two—approaching. Her sense of smell had heightened along with her other senses. Her vision had gained clarity, and she had no use for glasses to read. She even heard the beat of Raife's heart, along with the sound of Claude's, and the two mice in the nearby wall.

She knew it would take practice to filter all these new sensations so they didn't overwhelm. Raife had already explained it was a skill honed through the years. One would learn to ignore certain senses, focusing on one at a time. The tracking of a heartbeat always proved useful in hunting, but since Raife would provide her nourishment, she wouldn't have to worry too much about that.

"My friend is here with the other vampire Eva created."

They left her bedroom and reentered the store. There, a dark vampire—Spanish, judging from his looks—stood with another, a blond vampire with eyes that struck Yvette to the core. Such pain and loneliness reflected in those blue depths, she unconsciously extended her magic to him in comfort.

"*Amigo*, I heard of Eva's latest sin, creating another to feed her appetites. I wish to help." The Spaniard stepped to Yvette and took her hand with an Old World gallant charm. "Call me Vincente, *señorita.* I am at your service."

"Don't let this pirate fool you, love," Raife said. "He really is a wolf. In fact, the Spanish called him *El Lobo de Mar*, or the Sea Wolf."

The blond vampire fought her magical attempt to comfort him, as if wanting to feel the agony. What had happened to him to make him want to drown in pain?

"I'm Yvette." She introduced herself to him as Vincente and Raife began talking about the possibilities of Eva's location.

"Damon." He looked at her strangely and cocked his brow. "You're a fledgling."

"Yes, I was attacked and Raife made me..." She still hadn't fully accepted her change. It would likely take her a while before she came to grips with becoming a vampire. She couldn't help but wish the choice had been hers. She couldn't resent her lover for taking that choice from her, but as a modern woman, she would've liked to have had input in the decision.

The blond vampire suffered, the pain of loss filling his heart. He carried it with him like a scar upon his soul. "I can help you. I can feel your heartache." The man's pain was so palpable, Yvette could almost feel it in her own heart. Again she reached out to him with her magic, an attempt to sooth his wounded heart.

His eyes locked with hers, and he shook his head as he resisted her magical touch. "I loved once, but it wasn't meant to be. She died and left me behind to mourn. My pain is the price of falling in love with the forbidden."

"I'm sorry, Damon." She increased the magical caress to his soul.

"Your magic won't help me. I'm beyond anyone's help now." He turned from her, dismissing her sympathy. "Vince, Raife, we need to get going and search. Every moment of darkness Eva has, the stronger she will become."

Yvette grabbed her knapsack from behind the counter. "Yeah, let's get going."

Vince turned to Raife. "It'll be dangerous out there for a fledgling. I don't think she should go."

The comment angered Yvette. "You are not my master. I'll go along to help my mate."

"She'll be able to help." Then Raife added in a low voice, "You *can* help, right?"

"I have a few surprises in my bag of tricks. I might be able to cast a spell to slow her down so you gentlemen can do your duty. With her being ancient, she probably has her own magic and is much more powerful than I can handle." Judging from their discussions of Eva, Yvette knew they would need to kill the vampire. The idea, however, didn't thrill her and she didn't know how she would react. But having come face-to-face with many strange and bizarre things in her lifetimes, she knew that if a group of vampires said they had to destroy an evil vampire, she shouldn't question it.

"I'll just stay here and watch the home front," piped in Claude, jumping onto the counter next to the cash register.

"You do that, cat." Raife laughed as he strapped his scabbard to his hips. Sliding his sword into the sheath, he said at Vince's curious look, "Long story."

Chapter Seventeen

She traveled through the dark streets, wary of her surroundings. She could smell the dark creatures all around her. Nothing unusual. They were always around her. But tonight they were hunting her.

Fools. Did those vampires who fought and killed Michael really think they could find and defeat her? The young ones had no clue what they were pitting themselves against.

But still, she needed to be careful.

Eva had sensed one of her disloyal creations tracking her last night through the bayou. She would've stayed in the murky area, but her fledgling virgin had shivered too much from fright. Eva had been afraid to leave the girl in the swamp, especially when Damon searched so ruthlessly. So Eva took the weakened fledgling and locked her in an abandoned building off a dark alleyway, making sure her creation would remain waiting and hungry for her return. A newly turned vampire needed sustenance, and Eva would grant it only when she wanted to give it. She planned on using this fledgling for quite a while. It had been a long time since she'd tasted a woman's gifts. Men had been her primary staple of sexual pleasure, but from time to time, she liked variation in her menu. The female virgin's blood would continue to be a sweet treat indeed.

"You'll never get the chance to destroy the spirit of another," said a voice from her past.

"Damon, darling." Eva saw him approach in the dim alley, only steps away from the building sheltering her newest creation. "You never really complained when I drank from you. I seem to remember your kisses heating me like flaming coals on a winter's night."

"That was before you left me for your next conquest."

"I've always loved my creations. You're no different."

"All your creations? The hundreds of poor, helpless humans you transformed to satisfy your bloodthirsty needs?"

From the darkness, Eva felt the approach of more vampires set to destroy her. She laughed. "Think you can stop me, little Damon? Oh, and I see you finally met Raife. Now there is a lover I can never forget."

Raife, with a new lover at his side, never looked more tantalizing. Being in love suited him. Eva's eyes slid over the form of his witch-vampire. "I see you brought her along. You know she is a part of me too."

"Threaten my mate and you'll suffer long before death grants you release." Raife's eyes glowed with anger.

Eva wanted him. She really had felt something for the English pirate all those centuries ago. "You are a bunch of fools to try and take down your maker. Do you honestly think I'd let it happen?"

"I'd like to see you try and stop us from destroying you," Raife's mate retorted. She appeared spunky and courageous but not all that intelligent.

"Oh, I don't have to stop you," Eva said with a smile.

She called to her loyal servants. Eva wasn't as unprepared as they had likely expected.

* * * * *

The sound of flapping wings filled the dark alleyway as a flock of crows descended. They soared through the air, landed on the cobblestone street, perched along the iron fire escapes that clung to the sides of the brick buildings. Even more glared down from the rooftops. The black birds shifted shape. Soon, vampires of every race and background lined the alley behind the gloating Eva. An army of faithful vampires to do her battles.

Yvette's courage wavered.

Eva obviously enjoyed the moment. "Feeling so sure of yourselves now, my pets?"

Facing this army of servants, Yvette knew they would be lucky if they got out of this with their heads.

"I think we can even the score a bit," a voice quipped.

An Italian vampire, along with more vampires Yvette had never met, came up behind her and Raife. A red-haired woman dressed in a trench coat brandished a large, deadly looking machete. Another Italian smirked as he stood with his attractive mate, who was dressed like a gypsy with velvet scarves. But the large blond vampire with the air of sophistication and dominance, the one who had spoken, made Yvette shiver. He stepped through the street like he owned the town, closely followed by a large gray wolf.

"Lucius, you just don't know when you are beat, do you? Can't you see the odds are against you and your friends?"

"I never play the odds." The wolf at the vampire's side growled when he lifted his silver-tipped walking stick to polish the end. He seemed completely unconcerned of the vampires closing in around them. "If you don't call off your little batboys, I can guarantee they'll never see the moon rise again."

"My pets protect their mistress, just as your pet stands by you."

Yvette reached into her bag, formulating a plan.

"What are you doing?" Raife asked her in a whisper.

"Just stay inside the circle." She pulled out a large container of salt and flicked up the spout. "I can't stop them all, but I can make things a bit more in our favor."

Stepping around the group of friendly vampires, she quickly enclosed them in a circle of salt.

"I can't protect your blond friend and the wolf from my spell," she said in a hushed voice to Raife as she reached into her bag for two glass vials.

"I don't think any spell will affect Lucius. What are you going to do?"

"As I said, just stay inside the circle."

Eva paid no attention to Yvette, obviously dismissing her powers. But after Yvette's recent and powerful sexual gratification, her magic had grown strong. She murmured her plea to the goddesses, especially her patroness Bast, for the strength to overcome her foes.

Feeling the answer to her prayers, her body began to glow and she raised the arm holding the vials, tossing them outside the circle.

They hit the pavement, the blue glass shattering upon impact, the contents bursting into the air in a smoky cloud.

"Do you really think you ca—"

The cloud cut Eva's words short. It built into a storming presence, becoming larger and larger over the alley, rising into the air above the gathered vampires.

"Just don't move out of the circle," Yvette said to Raife and his friends as they watched in awe.

Then the storm broke. Eva's vampire army began to transform. They screamed and doubled over in pain as their bodies morphed and shifted.

"Damn you, witch!" Eva yelled. She retreated into the hoard of her vampires, now mewling, shrinking and taking on the characteristics of cats.

They shifted even smaller, becoming a disorganized, giant litter of kittens.

Eva ran. Lucius transformed into a great golden owl and flew in pursuit. His mate, however, affected by the spell, transformed into a kitten as well.

Raife turned to Yvette with a questioning look.

"The blond and Eva must be very powerful to resist the spell. But the others weren't so fortunate."

"How long will the spell last?" asked the redhead holding the machete.

"A few hours," Yvette gazed at the alley, now crowded with cute little fur balls, "but the vampires who are older won't be affected as long."

"Can we move now?" asked the Italian.

"Yes, we can go out of the circle now."

The male vampires shifted into various forms—a wolf, an owl, an eagle—and headed after Eva. The women, obviously fledglings in their own right and unable to shift as of yet, followed closely. The gypsy picked up the wolf-turned-kitten and ran after her mate.

Raife stepped to follow, but Yvette gently grasped his elbow.

"Aren't there enough going after Eva? Must you go?"

"Why? What is it?" he asked

"I'm…the spell took a lot out of me." She inched toward him and laid her head against his chest.

He held her in a loose embrace and sighed. "I can't hunt for Eva if you are weakened."

"My powers do need to be recharged."

He chuckled softly as he continued to hold her, stroking her hair with one hand. "Oh, torture."

As they turned away from the kittens scraping along the alley, trying to find hiding places, she asked, "What about these vampire kittens? The spell won't keep them like this for long."

"Eva is evil. Some of these vampires may be evil, but some may not. Killing them all would be like destroying all the fledglings Eva created—like me."

"But to let them live—"

"If any of them turn to the darkness and follow the ways of the *demoni,* the worst of our kind, then they will be dealt with when the time comes. Right now, they are merely victims of circumstance.

"And what of Eva? Do you think your friends will kill her?"

"Not sure. She is too slick to get caught easily. She may not be back in New Orleans for a long time."

"What about the new vampire she made?"

He stopped and gazed at the buildings lining the alley. "Damn it."

"Fear not, mon amigo. *I found where Eva was keeping the* señorita," Vince announced inside their minds. *"But it looks as if she is an escape artist. She must have gotten away during the day. I sense she hasn't been here for hours."*

"What are we going to do?" Yvette replied through her thoughts.

"I'll try to track her, but I think she probably left New Orleans."

"Where do you think she went?" Yvette asked aloud.

"Don't know. Where would a weak fledgling go?"

"Good question." Raife sounded annoyed at this twist of events.

"What makes you think she is weak?" Yvette asked.

"Because Eva starves her victims."

"She may not be starving now, though."

Vince sighed. *"Best follow the bloodless corpses, then…"*

They broke contact with Vincente as he proceeded to track the missing fledgling.

"Now, about recharging your powers," Raife said in a teasing tone. "Just how much recharging do you think you need?"

"Oh, a lot. May take hours…days. We'll have to try to have multiple orgasms for my powers to return to normal."

"Yep, this is just going to be torture, love."

"Raife?"

"Yes?"

"I'm glad it was you who answered the call. I think I fell in love with you the moment you stepped into my store." She wrapped her arms about his waist and peered up into his handsome face. His blue eyes sparkled with mischief and a deeper, tender emotion. "And, I love you for keeping me by your side, even if you had to make me a vampire. I didn't want to lose you so soon after finding you."

"It was quick for me too, Yvette. I knew you were my mate. I can't help but love you."

They sealed their eternal destiny together with a gentle kiss.

Also by Marianne LaCroix

Beast in My Bed
Bridesmaid and the Beast
Crossed Swords
Ellora's Cavemen: Dreams of the Oasis III (*anthology*)
Lady Sheba
Pirate's Mistress
Royal Bondage (*anthology*)
Scorpion King
Sea Hawk's Mistress

About the Author

ഋ

Multi-published author Marianne LaCroix lives in the American south in the land of cotton and mint juleps. She's an active member of the RWA in the ESPAN, GothRom, Passionate Ink, and First Coast Romance Writers chapters. She's had several recognitions for her writing including a Romantic Times BOOKClub Reviewer Choice nomination. Her tastes run to the alpha male with a dark streak in the form of a vampire, shape-shifter or other tortured-soul type. When not writing, Mari can be found with her twin toddler girls and her husband of eleven and half years.

Marianne welcomes comments from readers. You can find her website and email address on her author bio page at www.ellorascave.com.

Tell Us What You Think

We appreciate hearing reader opinions about our books. You can email us at Comments@EllorasCave.com.

Why an electronic book?

We live in the Information Age—an exciting time in the history of human civilization, in which technology rules supreme and continues to progress in leaps and bounds every minute of every day. For a multitude of reasons, more and more avid literary fans are opting to purchase e-books instead of paper books. The question from those not yet initiated into the world of electronic reading is simply: *Why?*

1. ***Price.*** An electronic title at Ellora's Cave Publishing and Cerridwen Press runs anywhere from 40% to 75% less than the cover price of the exact same title in paperback format. Why? Basic mathematics and cost. It is less expensive to publish an e-book (no paper and printing, no warehousing and shipping) than it is to publish a paperback, so the savings are passed along to the consumer.
2. ***Space.*** Running out of room in your house for your books? That is one worry you will never have with electronic books. For a low one-time cost, you can purchase a handheld device specifically designed for e-reading. Many e-readers have large, convenient screens for viewing. Better yet, hundreds of titles can be stored within your new library—on a single microchip. There are a variety of e-readers from different manufacturers. You can also read e-books on your PC or laptop computer. (Please note that Ellora's Cave does not endorse any specific brands.

You can check our websites at www.ellorascave.com or www.cerridwenpress.com for information we make available to new consumers.)

3. ***Mobility***. Because your new e-library consists of only a microchip within a small, easily transportable e-reader, your entire cache of books can be taken with you wherever you go.
4. ***Personal Viewing Preferences.*** Are the words you are currently reading too small? Too large? Too... ANNOYING? Paperback books cannot be modified according to personal preferences, but e-books can.
5. ***Instant Gratification.*** Is it the middle of the night and all the bookstores near you are closed? Are you tired of waiting days, sometimes weeks, for bookstores to ship the novels you bought? Ellora's Cave Publishing sells instantaneous downloads twenty-four hours a day, seven days a week, every day of the year. Our webstore is never closed. Our e-book delivery system is 100% automated, meaning your order is filled as soon as you pay for it.

Those are a few of the top reasons why electronic books are replacing paperbacks for many avid readers.

As always, Ellora's Cave and Cerridwen Press welcome your questions and comments. We invite you to email us at Comments@ellorascave.com or write to us directly at Ellora's Cave Publishing Inc., 1056 Home Avenue, Akron, OH 44310-3502.

2458079

Made in the USA